Kyla stood at the bedroom window and watched. Ethan ran like a professional athlete.

Or a man with the devil at his heels.

Even from this distance she could sense the grim determination that drove his long stride. She could almost feel the power and force of his body.

She'd begun watching out of concern, sure that such physical exertion would cause an injury, and then her gaze had turned almost greedy as she'd realised exactly what she was watching.

A male in his prime, at the peak of physical fitness. This was no city boy out for a guilt-driven exercise session. This was a man who regularly pushed his body to the limit.

She couldn't see his face, and yet she knew that his expression would be set and determined. Focused. Bleak?

Sensing that his run was more than a desire to raise his pulse-rate, Kyla turned away, giving him the privacy he so clearly craved, her curiosity well and truly piqued. Her own body suddenly stirred to an uncomfortable degree.

Dear Reader

The idea for a two-book series set on a fictitious Scottish island came to me when I was reading a magazine article on the challenges of life in a remote island community and a report on the problems faced by rural medical teams. I immediately imagined an island that contained all the things I love—a dramatic coastline, wonderful beaches, mountains and a long and interesting history. And so Glenmore Island was born.

Two characters immediately came to life for me. Kyla MacNeil is a feisty, independent, warm-hearted nurse who gives her heart and soul to her beloved island. Her life is wrapped up in friends and family: people she has known all her life. This is medicine at its most rewarding, with the team treating the whole patient within the community setting. Into that scenario comes reserved, brooding Dr Ethan Walker, a loner used to anonymity. He arrives on the island searching for answers, never expecting to stay, but he is seduced by spirited Kyla—and also by the charms of Glenmore Island.

Also in this book are a large cast of characters who live on the island and rely on their medical team to deliver the highest quality of medical care with little back-up. Being a boat or helicopter ride away from the nearest hospital requires resourcefulness, skill and confidence.

Glenmore offers something that is so often missing from our lives today: a sense of community, shared pride, and a commitment to enjoying nature and living well. It is certainly somewhere that I could live, and I hope by the time you've finished reading you would like to live there too.

I hope you enjoy Kyla's story and choose to visit Glenmore again in the second of the two books, which will be published next month.

Warmest wishes

Sarah x

A BRIDE
FOR GLENMORE

BY
SARAH MORGAN

MILLS & BOON
Pure reading pleasure

First published in Great Britain 2007
Large Print edition 2007
Harlequin Mills & Boon Limited,
Eton House, 18-24 Paradise Road,
Richmond, Surrey TW9 1SR

ISBN: 978 0 263 19371 8

Set in Times Roman 16¾ on 20 pt.
17-1107-48428

Printed and bound in Great Britain
by Antony Rowe Ltd, Chippenham, Wiltshire

Sarah Morgan trained as a nurse, and has since worked in a variety of health-related jobs. Married to a gorgeous businessman, who still makes her knees knock, she spends most of her time trying to keep up with their two little boys, but manages to sneak off occasionally to indulge her passion for writing romance. Sarah loves outdoor life, and is an enthusiastic skier and walker. Whatever she is doing, her head is always full of new characters and she is addicted to happy endings.

CHAPTER ONE

THE ferry docked in the early morning.

It was the start of summer, a fresh June day with plenty of cloud in an angry sky, and Ethan stood by the white rail with the other foot passengers, his eyes on the shore. The cool wind whipped playfully at his dark hair as if to remind him that this was remote Scotland and that meant that even summer weather was unpredictable.

Despite the early hour, the harbour was already busy and people were milling around the dock, buying fish straight from the boats and passing the time of day. From his vantage point high on the boat, Ethan could see a cluster of cottages, a café, a gift shop and an old-fashioned greengrocer with fruit and vegetables artfully arranged to draw the eye and the customer. From the harbour the road rose, snaking upwards and then curving out of sight along the coast.

Even without the benefit of local knowledge he knew where that road led. In fact, he felt as though he knew every contour of Glenmore island, even though he'd never been here before.

As if to remind himself of his reason for being there, he slipped a hand into his pocket and fingered the letter. He'd done the same thing so many times before that the notepaper was crumpled and the writing barely legible in parts, but he didn't need to read it because he'd long since committed the contents to memory.

The description in the letter had been so detailed, the words so vivid that already the island felt familiar. In his mind he'd felt the cold chill of the wild, inhospitable mountains that clustered in the centre of the island and he'd walked the rocky shores that had sent so many ships to their doom. In his imagination, he'd sailed the deep loch and scrambled on the ruins of the ancient castle, the site of a bloody battle between Celts and Vikings centuries earlier. Glenmore had a turbulent past and a rich history thanks to the fierce determination of the locals to maintain their freedom.

Freedom.

Wasn't that what everyone wanted? It was certainly one of the reasons he was there. He needed to escape from the throttling grip of his past.

Suddenly Ethan wanted to sprint to the top of the highest point and breathe in the air and then he wanted to plunge into the icy waters of the Atlantic Ocean and swim with the porpoises that were reputed to inhabit this area. It felt good to escape from external pressures and the expectations of others and he had to remind himself that being there wasn't about escape, it was about discovery.

He'd come for answers.

And he intended to find those answers.

If he happened to enjoy being in this wild, remote corner of Scotland, then that was a bonus.

Ethan felt a sudden lift in his spirits and the feeling was as surprising as it was unexpected.

Well-meaning colleagues and friends had told him that he was mad to bury himself all the way up here on a Scottish Island. With qualifications like his, he should have been returning to Africa with all its medical challenges, or working at the renowned London teaching hospital where he'd trained. *They'd warned him that Island life would be dull.* Nothing but in-growing toenails and varicose veins—old ladies moaning about the pressures of advancing age. He would be bored within a week.

A faint smile touched Ethan's classically handsome face. It remained to be seen whether they were right about the lack of job satisfaction, but at the moment it wasn't boredom he was feeling. It was exhilaration.

And a deep sadness for the loss of something precious and irreplaceable.

He breathed in deeply and felt the salty air sting his lungs. It was time to leave the ferry.

Time to begin. He started to move away from the rail and then he paused, his eye caught by a tall, slender girl who was weaving her way through the groups of people hovering on the dock, awaiting the arrival of the ferry. She walked with bounce and energy, as if she had a million things to do and not enough time, returning greetings with a wave and a few words, hardly breaking stride as she made for the boat. Her hair was long and loose, her smile wide and friendly, and she carried a large sloppy bag over one shoulder. Anchoring it firmly, she leapt onto the ramp of the ferry with the grace of a gazelle.

Not a *girl,* he saw immediately, but a young woman, perhaps in her early twenties, and everything about her was vital and energetic.

The wind drew the conversation upwards.

'Hey, Kyla, you can't come on without a ticket.' The ferryman strolled towards her, a grin on his weathered face, and the girl reached up and planted a kiss on his cheek, her eyes twinkling.

'I've come for my deliveries, Jim. Logan

ordered some equipment from the mainland and I've orders to collect it before breakfast, along with the post and the new doctor.'

Ethan frowned. *Kyla*. The letter had mentioned Kyla and finally he was putting a face to the name. And it was a lovely face. *So lovely that he found that he couldn't look away.*

The ferryman was hauling a sack onto the dock. His boots were dusted with sand and there were streaks of oil on his arms. 'The new doctor?'

'That's right. We ordered him from the mainland, too.' The woman stooped to help him with the sack. 'He'd better be good quality. If not, he's going right back. My poor brother needs help in the surgery almost as much as he needs a decent night's sleep.'

Jim snorted. 'Not likely to get it, with that bairn of his almost a year old.'

Ethan watched as Kyla's pretty smile faltered for a moment. 'He's doing all right. My aunt's been really busy at the café so one of the Foster girls has been helping him for the past few weeks. She's good with the baby. It's working out well.'

'Until she starts building up her hopes and hearing wedding bells, like everyone else who goes near that brother of yours.' Jim reached behind him and picked up a parcel and a bag of post. 'I suppose this is what you're after. You're up early for a girl who went to bed late. It was a good party last night. Don't you ever lie in?'

She dropped the post into the bag on her shoulder and lifted the parcel carefully, balancing it in her arms. 'Find me someone decent to lie in with, Jim, and I'll be happy to stay in bed. Until then I may as well work. Somebody has to keep everyone on this island healthy and strong.'

'Any time you want company in that lonely old cottage of yours, just say the word.'

Kyla opened her mouth to reply but the words didn't come and the beautiful smile faded as she stared at something.

It took a moment for Ethan to realise that he

was that something. And another moment for him to realise that he was staring back and that he'd walked almost to her side without even noticing that he'd done so. He'd been drawn to her and the knowledge unsettled him. He was accustomed to being in control of his reactions, especially when it came to women.

Irritated with himself, he kept his tone cool. 'I heard you mention that you're meeting the new doctor. I'm Dr Walker. Ethan Walker.' He watched her face for signs of recognition, relieved when he saw none. *Why would there be?* It wasn't a name she'd know. And he had no intention of enlightening her. Not yet. He needed time to establish himself. Time to assess the situation without the complications that revealing his identity would inevitably arouse.

He watched as the wind picked up a strand of her blonde hair and blew it across her face.

'You're Dr Walker?' Her gaze was frank and appraising with no trace of either shyness or flirtation. She made no secret of the fact he was under scrutiny and he had the strangest feeling that if she hadn't liked what she'd seen she would have sent him back on the ferry to the mainland.

A strange heat spread through his body and he gave a faint smile.

His lifestyle wasn't compatible with long, meaningful relationships and he was careful to avoid them, but that didn't mean he wasn't capable of appreciating feminine appeal when it was standing in front of him.

At another time, in another place he might have done something about the powerful thud of attraction that flared between them, but he reminded himself that romance would only tangle the already complicated.

He tried to analyse the strength of his reaction— tried to provide a logical explanation for the primitive thud of lust that tore through his body.

It was true that she was striking, but he'd been with women more beautiful and more sophisticated—women to whom grooming was a full-time preoccupation. No one could describe Kyla's appearance as groomed. She was as wild as the island she inhabited, her hair falling loose over her shoulders in untamed waves and her face free of make-up. But her smile was wide and her eyes sparkled with an enthusiasm for life that was infectious. She looked like a woman who knew the meaning of the word happiness. An optimist. A woman who was going to grab life round the throat and enjoy every last second.

Aware that he was still staring, Ethan reminded himself firmly that his reasons for coming to the nethermost reaches of Scotland didn't include a need for female company.

'I'm Kyla MacNeil. Logan's sister.' She balanced the parcel on one arm and extended a hand. 'Welcome to Glenmore, Dr Walker. If you come with me, I'll take you straight up to the surgery and then I'll show you your new home and help get you settled in.'

'You're Logan's sister?' Ethan stared down

into her blue eyes and searched for a resemblance. 'He talked about a little sister…'

'That's me. I'm twenty-five years old but that's six years less than him so I suppose that makes me his little sister. Are you going to shake this hand of mine, Dr Walker? Because if not, I'll put it away.'

Wondering why he was at a loss with a woman when he'd always considered himself experienced with her sex, Ethan shook her hand and nodded to Jim. 'Thanks for the lift. I'll be seeing you around.'

'If you're the new Island doctor, I hope you won't. The only time I plan to see you is in the pub or when I'm waving you goodbye as you leave this place.' Jim stepped back as the last of the cars clanked its way down the ramp and onto the quay. 'I intend to stay healthy.'

'Talking of which, how's that diet of yours going?' Kyla clutched the parcel to her chest and Jim pulled a face.

'Ever since she talked to you about what I

should be eating, all Maisie seems to cook these days is fish and porridge. No bacon and eggs and I haven't seen a piece of cheese since the sun last shone, and that's a while ago. Life's just miserable. The only good thing is that Logan's stopped nagging me because he's very pleased with my cholesterol. It's come right down on that new drug.'

'That would be the statin he switched you to. Glad to hear it's working. Well, we need to go. I need to get to the surgery or Logan will be grumbling. Take care of yourself, Jim. The forecast for the end of the week is storms.'

Jim gave a grunt and watched as the last car clattered its way over the ramp and onto the island. 'Wouldn't be Glenmore if we didn't have storms.'

She turned to Ethan. 'Didn't you bring a car?'

'I've been working abroad until recently. I took the train but my car is being delivered later today. I gave them the address of the surgery.'

'In that case, you'll need a lift to the surgery. It's too far to walk.'

Ethan shifted his case into the other hand. 'Let me carry the box for you.'

'All right. I'm not one to reject a chivalrous gesture, even in the twenty-first century.' She relinquished the parcel and adjusted the bag on her shoulder. 'Don't drop it. It's a new defibrillator. One of those ones that talks to you, although, knowing my brother, if it starts to give him instructions he'll probably argue with it.'

Ethan took the parcel from her and followed her along the quay, watching the way everyone converged on her.

'Kyla.' An elderly woman crossed the street to speak to her. 'I read that leaflet you gave me about strengthening your bones…'

'Glad to hear it, Mrs Porter.' She paused, her smile friendly. 'All OK?'

'Oh, yes. It advised you to walk more and lift weights. I'm a bit too old for the gym, so I filled some empty milk bottles with water and I've been using those.'

'Great idea. Well, if you have any questions

you can find me in surgery and we can have a really good chat. And don't forget to speak to Evanna about doing her exercise class.'

She walked on a bit further before she was stopped by one of the fishermen who was untangling his net. 'Nurse MacNeil—I need to have those stitches of mine taken out.'

'How's the leg feeling?'

'Sore.'

She nodded. 'It was a nasty cut. You need to keep it up when you're resting. Pop in on Friday and I'll take the stitches out and take another look at it. If you need antibiotics, I can have a word with Logan.'

She walked on, somehow managing to acknowledge everyone's greeting in a friendly manner while avoiding lengthy conversation.

Ethan watched in silent admiration, trying to imagine something similar happening in London and failing. In London everyone kept their eyes forward and went about their own business. 'You know everyone.'

'This is an island, Dr Walker. Everyone knows everyone.' She scraped her unruly hair out of her eyes and lifted an eyebrow in his direction. 'Is that going to be a problem for you?'

'Why would it be?'

Her glance was assessing. 'You're a city boy and the one thing that you can guarantee in a big, soulless city is anonymity. And that suits some people. Not everyone wants folks knowing their business.'

A city boy.

Ethan thought about the places he'd worked in, the dust, the heat and the sheer weight of human suffering. *She had no idea.* Oh, yes, he'd experienced anonymity. The sort where you shouted and no one listened.

Kyla lengthened her stride, nodded to an elderly woman who passed and then paused to stroke a baby who was cooing in a pushchair. 'Can't believe he's two months now, Alice. Make sure you remember to bring him to clinic for his injections.' They moved on and Ethan watched as she pulled a set of keys out of her jacket pocket.

'Anonymity is one thing but time off is another. How do you switch off and keep people at a distance?'

'On the whole people are pretty good about not invading our privacy. If I'm wearing lipstick and heels and have a drink in my hand, they know better than to expect me to discuss their haemorrhoids.' She juggled the keys in her hand. 'But it's definitely a close community and that can be a good thing or a bad thing, depending on the person you are or what you happen to be doing at the time. If you're not careful you can find yourself doing impromptu consultations on every street corner. Not that I mind in some cases, but generally speaking I want to feel I have a life outside work. We need to get a move on. The surgery is ten minutes' drive from here, in the village.'

He glanced around him. 'This isn't the village?'

'No, Dr Walker. This is the quay. People live

dotted all over the place, which makes it a laugh a minute when you have an urgent house call, as you will soon discover.' She stopped by a tiny car in a deep shade of purple. 'Hop in. We'll go to the surgery and I'll introduce you to my brother and then I'll drop you at your cottage before I go back to my clinic.'

'This is your car?' He glanced at it in disbelief and she scowled at him across the top of the car, the expression in her blue eyes suddenly dangerous.

'If you're thinking of making a derogatory remark about the colour, then I advise against it. I happen to be very attached to my car. And so should you be, Dr Walker, because if it weren't for my car, you'd be walking up that hill with your luggage as we speak.'

Even on such a short acquaintance, he could see that she was a woman with a warm heart and a fiery temper. The combination was intriguing. For the first time in months he found himself fighting the desire to smile. 'Would you believe

me if I told you that lurid purple is my favourite colour?'

'Very funny.' She glared at him for a moment
and then grinned. 'All right, I'll be honest. I got
it at a knock-down price from the mainland.
Apparently no one else liked the colour.'

'You astonish me.'

'Sarcasm doesn't become you, Dr Walker. The
boot's open if you want to get rid of that suitcase.'
She slid into the driver's seat and he somehow
jammed his suitcase into the tiny boot and then
climbed in next to her, wincing as he tried to
fold his six foot three frame into the tiny vehicle.

'It may be an awful colour,' he muttered,
easing the door shut, 'but at least it's roomy.'

'Are you being rude about my car?' She
glanced towards him and burst out laughing.
'You look ridiculous.'

'It's the car that's ridiculous.'

'The car is fine, but you're too big for it.'

Ethan winced and tried to ease his legs into a
more comfortable position. 'I'm aware of that

fact.' He shifted down in the seat to give himself more head room and found his knees under his chin. 'Well, this is comfortable. Drive on. Wherever we're going, we'd better get there quickly or I'll need physiotherapy at the end of the journey and I don't suppose that's available on an island this remote.'

'Don't you believe it. Glenmore may be remote but we've a thriving population here. Physio is Evanna's division. Especially massage. She's great with crying babies and pretty good with moaning adults, too.' She started the engine, checked her rear-view mirror and started up the coast road at a frightening pace.

'Evanna?' Ethan wondered how a car so small could go so fast. 'I heard you mention her to the lady who spoke to you back on the quay. She's the other practice nurse?'

'That's right. We each have different responsibilities. Evanna is a midwife as well as a practice nurse and she's had some basic physio training.

We all do a bit of everything if we can. It saves folks travelling all the way to the mainland.'

To one side of him the coast flashed past and he had a glimpse of rocky coves and sandy beaches. The island had a dramatic history, he recalled, with a good number of wrecks littering the seabed. He stared out to sea, his mind wandering. There were so many questions he wanted to ask but to do so would reveal too much so instead he turned back to look at her, studying her profile. From this angle he could see that her nose turned up slightly and that her eyelashes were long and thick. She had a sweet face, he decided. A happy face. There were no lines. No shadows. Nothing to suggest that life had sent her anything that she couldn't handle.

'You're staring at me, Dr Walker, and it's putting me off my driving.'

'Then I'll keep my eyes straight ahead.' He gave a faint smile. 'Given the proximity of this road to the edge of the cliff, I certainly wouldn't want to put you off.'

'I've lived here all my life. There's not a kink in this road that I don't know. And I'm a jack of all trades. I'm the dietician, the asthma specialist and the diabetes nurse. I'm trained in family planning but we're not exactly encouraging that at the moment because the population of the island is dwindling. If anyone comes to me for contraception, I send them away to have more sex and make a baby. We need babies on the Island or the next thing you know they'll be taking away a doctor and trying to close the school.'

Despite the dark clouds in his head, Ethan found himself laughing. 'Well, that's a novel approach to family planning. Are you serious? Is the school under threat of closure?'

'No, not yet.' She glanced towards him with a quick smile. 'Actually, this is a thriving, busy island and we're doing all right. But populations dwindle. It's a fact in rural areas like this. People find the life hard and they leave for the bright lights of the big cities. And they don't come back. They marry a mainlander like you and have their babies somewhere else.'

She changed gear and took a corner at an alarming speed.

'Do you always drive this fast?'

'I do everything fast. It means I can get through twice as much in the day, which is a definite advantage in a place like this. But that's enough about me. What brings you here? What are you running from, Dr Walker?'

He felt his body tense. 'Why would I be running from anything?'

'Because mainlanders don't generally choose to spend their summer up here in the wilds unless they're running from something,' she said cheerfully. 'Unless they're locals, people come here for space and to regroup. Was it work or something more personal? Love?'

His head started to throb. He'd expected questions. He just hadn't expected them this quickly. *And he hadn't prepared his answers.* 'Are you always this direct?'

'On an island, it's impossible to keep secrets.' She opened the window a crack and the breeze blew in and lifted her hair. 'They have a habit of following you. Better to get it all out in the open.'

Ethan stared at her profile and then turned his head away to stare out of his own window. *If she knew his secret, she'd probably stop the car and push him off the cliff.* 'I'm not in the habit of talking about my sex life.'

'Right.' She shifted her grip on the steering-wheel. 'But I wasn't asking about your sex life, I was asking about your love life.'

It occurred to him that she would have got on well with his last girlfriend. *You don't have a heart, Ethan. You're not capable of intimacy.*

'I'm here because you advertised for a doctor. Logan told me he needed help.'

'He does need help. But that wouldn't be enough to attract a mainlander to a place like Glenmore. And Logan told me that you're a hotshot. First in everything. Top of your class.'

'Being a good doctor isn't about exam results.'

'Well, it's good to know we agree on something.' She shifted gear and slowed down to take a corner. 'Anyway, we're just pleased to have you here. It's been a tough few months. I don't know whether Logan mentioned it but he lost his wife almost a year ago.'

Ethan stiffened and the throb in his head intensified. 'Yes,' he said quietly, forcing his body to relax. 'He mentioned it.'

'It was a hideous time.' Kyla's voice was soft and her hands tight on the wheel. 'Awful.'

Ethan felt the sickness rise inside him. 'How did she die?'

'Having the baby.' Kyla shook her head slowly. 'It seems so wrong, doesn't it? In this day and age to die having a baby. You read about maternal mortality rates but you don't actually think it's going to happen to anyone you know. You think that if you monitor carefully, everything will be all right. But it wasn't all right. And I know Logan still blames himself even though he did absolutely everything that could have been done. She had an undiagnosed cardiac condition.'

Ethan took a deep breath. 'And how's he managing with the little girl? It must be difficult.'

'How did you know they had a girl?' She shot him a surprised look, her blue eyes narrowed. 'Did I mention it?'

'Logan mentioned it,' Ethan said, correcting his mistake swiftly. 'Kirsty. Eleven months.'

'That's right. She's a sweetie. She isn't walking yet but her crawling could earn her a speeding ticket and she's into everything. Gives us all grey hairs. And Logan manages. He's a great father and he has a lot of help from the islanders. One of my aunts runs the café on the quay along with one of my cousins, and they often take Kirsty for him during the day.'

'*One* of your aunts?'

'My grandmother was obviously preserving the future of the island. My mother was one of six.' She grinned at him. 'I have five aunts and eleven first cousins. Some of them have moved away, of course, but most of them still live on the island, which is handy for Logan. He hasn't cooked himself a meal for months, lucky creature. It's useful to have family around, isn't it?'

It was a concept so alien to Ethan that he found it impossible to answer. To avoid the inevitable questions, he took the conversation off on a different tangent. 'You don't like cooking?'

'Not one of my skills, but I do like eating.'

'And Logan has worked here since he finished his training?'

'No. He worked in London for a while, gaining the experience he needed to be able to work in a place like this. Out here it's the real thing, Dr Walker. No back-up. It takes skill and confidence to deal with that. Most islanders escape for a while just to see if the grass is greener on the other side and when they discover that it isn't…' She gave a slight shrug of her shoulders as she flicked the indicator and turned the car into a small car park '…they come back again. We're here. This is Glenmore Medical Centre.'

It was larger than Ethan had expected, a modern building with clean lines and glass, attached to a stunning house, painted white and with several balconies that faced towards the sea. 'Your brother lives here.'

'Yes. The surgery is attached to the house and, of course, people take all sorts of liberties, banging on his door when he's in the bath and that sort of thing.' She smiled and switched off the engine. 'But he loves it here.'

'From what I've heard, your brother is well qualified. He could have worked anywhere.'

'That's right. He could.' She reached into the back seat for her bag, her movements swift and decisive. 'And he chose to work here, where he grew up—where his talents really count for something. On Glenmore you're not one of hundreds of doctors, you're the only one. Sometimes you're the only person who can make a difference. You're truly needed.'

'And you love it.'

'Oh, yes.' She pulled the bag into her lap and

then paused, a wistful smile on her face. 'As it happens, I've tried leaving. I've tried living in other places but they never feel right. When I'm here on Glenmore, somehow everything falls into place and I know I'm home.'

'It must be nice to feel that way about a place.'

'Everyone has somewhere that feels like home,' she said cheerfully as she opened the car door. 'Where is it for you? London?'

Ethan sat in silence, thinking about the question. 'That depends on your definition of home. Is it the place where you were born or the place where you grew up?'

She paused with her on the door as she considered the question. 'It's not necessarily either. Home is the place where you feel completely comfortable. You are there and suddenly you can't remember why you ever left because it's the only place you really want to be.'

Ethan studied her face for a moment. 'Then I don't think I have a home,' he said quietly, 'because I've never felt that way about anywhere.'

CHAPTER TWO

KYLA opened the boot and removed the box, trying not to stare as Ethan Walker uncurled his powerful body from the front seat of her car and stretched.

All the way in the car she'd been aware of him. Aware of the shadow of stubble darkening his jaw, of long, masculine leg brushing against hers and the long, searching looks he kept casting in her direction. She'd felt those looks— *felt him looking at her*—and something about the burning intensity of his gaze had disturbed her so badly that she'd driven fast to keep the journey as short as possible.

Her nerve endings had snapped tight and she'd

been breathlessly conscious of every movement he'd made during the short journey.

She knew everyone who lived on the island. She was used to men who were safe and predictable. And she sensed that Ethan Walker was neither.

When her brother had given her the lowdown on the new island doctor, she'd conjured up a vision of a bespectacled, wiry academic who'd spent his life looking down a microscope and seeing patients from the other side of a large desk.

She hadn't expected to be knocked off her feet by the sight of him.

It wasn't just the handsome face and the athletic body that made it hard not to stare at him. It was the air of quiet confidence and the dark, almost brooding quality that surrounded him. She sensed that his emotions were buried deep inside him. Were those emotions responsible for the hard, cynical gleam in his eyes?

And what was he doing up here in the wilds of Scotland?

He'd evaded her question but she wasn't a

fool. If Logan was right, then Ethan had been on the fast track. Hadn't he said that Ethan had been the youngest consultant they'd ever had in the hospital? A single-minded, ambitious over-achiever? Why would a man with that sort of career ahead of him suddenly leave it to work in a backwater?

It had to be something to do with his love life.

Hadn't he ignored the question when she'd asked it? Which was entirely typical of a man, she thought to herself, because since when did men ever talk about their feelings? They were all completely hopeless.

She slammed the boot shut, deciding that it would be interesting to get some answers. And interesting to spend some time with him.

The thought surprised her because it had been a long time since she'd found herself wanting to spend time with a man.

The problem with island life, she reflected as she slipped the postbag onto her shoulder, was that she knew absolutely everyone. There were no surprises. She wasn't suddenly going to look at Nick Hillier, the island policeman, and feel a hot flush coming on. She wasn't going to go to bed dreaming of Alastair and his fishing boat. She knew everyone on the island as well as she knew her family.

But Ethan—Ethan was a surprise. A surprise that promised to make the long days of summer more interesting than usual.

Her mouth curved into a smile as she anticipated the days ahead.

It would be interesting, she decided, to find out more about him.

She pushed open the surgery door.

Her brother was sprawled in a chair at the reception desk, hitting keys on the computer. 'I've a full list here, Kyla. Did you book these in?'

'And good morning to you, too.' Her eyes scanned her brother's face, looking for signs of strain. Tiredness. Logan was the toughest person she knew but all the same she worried about him. He was doing all right, she decided. She was proud of him. 'Have you been here all night?'

'It certainly feels like it.' He pushed the chair away from the computer and stretched. His hair was dark and touched the edge of his collar, but his eyes were as blue as hers. 'I need every second of the day to see these patients. We have to stop booking them in.'

Kyla threw him an exasperated look. 'Well what do you expect me to do, you idiot? Tell them to go away and pick another day to be ill?'

'Nice to get some proper respect around here,' Logan drawled, but there was a twinkle in his eyes. 'I'm just pointing out that there's only one of me and at the moment I'm spread rather thinly.'

Kyla slammed the post down on the reception desk. 'Well, despite what you may think, I don't spend my time going round the Island drumming up business for your surgeries. Can I help it if people think you're the answer to their problems? Anyway, there isn't just one of you any more.' She turned with a wave of her hand. 'I brought you reinforcements from the ferry, Dr Ethan Walker. I expect you already know that because he's the only stranger that stepped off the ferry this morning so I dare say the jungle drums have been beating for the last half an hour. Treat him well and perhaps he'll help you with your surgery.'

'Ethan—pleased to meet you.' Logan straightened and the two men shook hands while Kyla tilted her head to one side and studied them both. They had a similar physique and yet they were entirely different. Both dark, both tall, both broad-shouldered, but the resemblance ended there. While her brother looked rough and rugged, as though he'd just strode off the hills, Ethan was smooth and slick. *City slick*, Kyla thought as she turned away and started stacking the post neatly for Janet, their receptionist, to open later. He was a man who looked…she searched for the right term…*expensive*.

And he probably wasn't going to last five minutes in a place like Glenmore.

The two men were deep in conversation when the phone rang. Reaching over the desk, Kyla lifted the receiver, her hair falling forward.

'Glenmore Medical Centre.' Her voice was bright and friendly and she ignored a look from Logan that warned her that trying to cram another patient onto his morning list would put her life at risk. 'Hello, Janet! How are you doing?' She straightened and pulled a face. 'Oh, no—that's awful! I'm so sorry to hear that. Don't move her. Logan will be right over.'

She replaced the receiver to find Logan gazing at her in disbelief. 'Remind me to fire you and replace you with a moody, scary battleaxe who frightens away patients. If you've booked me a house call two minutes before my morning surgery starts then I'm going to strangle you with my bare hands,' he growled. 'What do you think I am? Superhuman?'

'A good doctor.' Kyla scribbled the details on a scrap of paper and then walked across and gave him a swift kiss on the cheek. 'A good but exceptionally *moody* doctor. That was our Janet. She popped round to check on her mum this morning and found her collapsed on the floor.'

'Gladys?' Logan's frown changed to a look of concern and Kyla thrust a piece of paper into his hands.

'You see? You care really, you know you do. You just hide it well. This isn't going to wait, Logan. She needs to be seen right away.'

'I have surgery—I can't be in two places at once.'

'Well, I think the place you need to be is with Mrs Taylor. Janet thinks she's broken her leg. You go. I'll keep the patients happy. Evanna and I will see the ones that we can and the others will just have to wait.' Kyla waved a hand towards the door. 'Go forth and heal, oh great one. I can sing and dance and generally entertain them while you swan off like a knight in shining armour.'

'I'll start your surgery.' Ethan stepped forward, cool and unflustered, watching the exchange between them with puzzled curiosity. 'Why not?'

Logan ran a hand over the back of his neck. 'Because you've been travelling all night? Because you must need a shower and a rest? Because you don't know the patients or the island? How many more reasons do you need?'

Ethan gave a faint smile. 'I'm used to travelling and the shower and the rest can wait. As for not knowing the patients or the island…' he gave a dismissive shrug of his broad shoulders '…I don't see why that should that be a problem. Presumably Kyla's on hand if I need help. Keep your mobile on. If I have any questions, I'll call you.'

'All right, then. If you're sure.' Without further argument Logan reached for his bag. 'If she's fractured her hip, I'm going to need the air ambulance, Kyla. I'll call you.'

'You do that.' Kyla watched her brother stride through the door and then picked up a set of keys. 'All right, Dr Walker. Looks like you're on duty. I'll show you your room then I'll fetch you a cup of coffee. Hopefully that will see you through until we have time for something more—' She didn't finish her sentence because the surgery door crashed open and a large man staggered in. His face was pale and shone with sweat, his hand pressed against his chest.

'Doug!' Kyla was by his side in a flash, her arm sliding around him in an instinctive offer of support. 'What's happened? Are you ill?'

'Pain.' His face was contorted in agony and tiny drops of sweat clung to his forehead. 'Terrible pain in my chest. I was down in the basement, shifting crates of beer, when I started to feel funny. A bit sick, to be honest. Then it hit me all of a sudden. It's like an elephant on my chest.'

'Can we lay him down somewhere?'

'In the consulting room.'

Ethan took the man's arm and he and Kyla guided him down the corridor into the room. 'Let's get you up on the couch, Mr...?'

'McDonald,' Kyla said quickly, raising the back of the couch and helping the patient to lie down. 'Doug McDonald. Fifty-six years of age, been treated for hypertension for the past three years. He's taking beta blockers, an ace inhibitor and a statin.'

Ethan lifted a brow as he took Doug's pulse and reached for a stethoscope. 'You know every patient's history by heart?'

'Small community, Dr Walker. What do you need?'

'Start with oxygen?'

'There's a cylinder to your right with a mask already attached, and I expect you'll want to put a line in. I'll fetch you the tray.' Brisk and efficient, she reached into the cupboard, removed the tray and placed it on the trolley next to him. 'Just breathe normally through that mask, Doug. That's great. I'll squeeze while you find a vein, Dr Walker.' She put her hands around Doug's arm, watching while Ethan stroked the back of his hand, searching for a vein.

'Do we have the facility to start an IV?'

'Of course. I'll run a bag of fluid through for you.'

'You have good veins, Doug.' He cleaned the

skin, inserted the cannula with the ease of someone who had performed the same procedure successfully a million times before. Kyla gave a faint nod of approval and released her grip on Doug's arm.

'You're doing fine, Doug. Dr Walker will soon have you feeling better. I'll get the notes up on the screen for you,' she said to Ethan. 'That way you'll be able to see what Logan has been doing.' She moved over to the desk, flicked on the computer, crossed the room and grabbed the ECG machine from the corner. 'That computer will just take a minute to wake up.'

Doug gave a grunt of pain, his hand on the mask. 'I was always afraid that this might happen. It's why I tried to lose weight. I managed to stop smoking but I just ate more.' He grimaced and leaned back against the pillow as Ethan connected a bag of fluid. 'I've been trying, really I have. But it's so hard.'

'You've been doing brilliantly, Doug, you know that. Don't worry about it now,' Kyla said quickly, wrapping the blood-pressure cuff around his other arm. 'We just need to find out what's happening.' She checked his BP, showed Ethan the result and he gave her a nod.

'Can we do a 12-lead ECG?'

'Already on it.' Kyla quickly stuck the pads onto the patient and applied the chest leads and limb leads. 'Just hang in there, Douglas, you're going to be fine. Dr Walker is a real whiz kid from the mainland. People usually pay a fortune to see him, but you're getting him free so this is your lucky day.'

She was aware of the sardonic lift of Ethan's dark brows but chose to ignore him. This was her territory, she reminded herself. There was no way she was going to allow herself to be intimidated by a locum doctor, no matter how slick and handsome.

Doug closed his eyes and gave a wan smile. 'It doesn't feel like my lucky day, hen.'

Kyla felt her heart twist at the endearment. *She'd known Doug since she'd been a child.* 'Of course it's lucky because I'm on duty,' she said lightly, switching on the machine. 'If you had to be ill then you've done it in the right place. You're going to be OK, Doug.' She chatted away in a steady, reassuring voice and then looked up as the door opened and a dark-haired girl in a blue uniform hurried into the room.

'I just drove past Logan breaking the speed limit on the coast road and, judging from the look on his face, I thought you might need some help here.' Her eyes were gentle and concerned and her ponytail swung as she moved her head. 'Doug? What have you been doing to yourself?'

'This is Ethan Walker, the new GP. Ethan, this is Evanna, the other island nurse. Logan's gone to see Janet's mother who's had a fall and our Doug here is having nasty chest pains. Can you call the air ambulance?' Kyla glanced up at her friend and colleague and used her eyes to transmit the message that the request was urgent. 'Whatever happens, we're going to need to transfer Doug to the mainland. Doug, I need to call your wife and let her know what's happening. Is she home?'

Evanna slid out of the room without argument and Kyla felt a flicker of relief. She knew she could trust her friend to get the air ambulance to the island as quickly as possible.

'No.' Douglas turned his head, his face pale and sweaty and his voice urgent. 'You're not to worry Leslie. She's got enough on her mind at the moment with our Andrea going through a rebellious phase. She doesn't need this. I'm having a heart attack, I know I am. It'll be too much for her.'

'She loves you, Doug,' Kyla said firmly, starting the machine and watching the trace. She didn't like what she saw but she was careful not to let her worry show on her face. *But she was definitely calling his wife.* 'You're a partnership. A team. What do you think she'd say when she discovers that you've flown off on a mini-break to the mainland and left her here?'

ST elevation, she thought to herself, studying the pattern. She'd seen it often enough in her short time in A and E.

Doug gave a wan smile and shook his head. 'She's always on at me to leave the island for a break.'

'Well, there you are, then.' Kyla stood to one side so that Ethan could watch the trace. 'There's ST segment elevation in two leads. I expect you'll want to give him heparin and reteplase. I'll get it ready.'

Ethan looked at her and she saw approval and a flicker of surprise in his eyes. 'Do we have morphine and GTN spray?'

'Of course.' The question amused her. So he thought he was working in a backwater, did he? She unlocked the drug cupboard, found what she needed and prepared it, listening as he talked to Doug.

'I'm afraid the ECG shows that you're right about the heart attack, Doug. Probably caused by a blood clot in one of the vessels leading to your heart.' His tone was calm and steady. 'I'm going to give you a drug that will break it down.'

'One of those clot-busters I've been reading about?'

'That's right. We need to get the blood flowing back through that artery for you. Before I give it, I need to ask you a few questions.'

Doug winced, his face pale behind the mask. 'I ought to warn you that I hate quiz night at the pub. I never go. If you're about to start on capital cities, you can forget it. I left school at sixteen and went out on my father's boat.'

Ethan smiled. 'You don't suffer from any bleeding disorders? Haven't had surgery lately?' He asked a series of rapid questions and then took the drugs from Kyla. 'How long does the air ambulance usually take to arrive and where do they land? I'm not sure he's stable enough to travel.'

'The paramedics are skilled and you can go with him. They carry a defibrillator, along with all the other gear you're likely to need.'

Ethan administered the drug carefully. 'And they can fly here?'

'Oh, yes, providing the weather is all right, and today it should be fine.' Kyla took the empty syringe from him and disposed of it with swift efficiency. 'We need to call the hospital and fill out details for the transfer.'

'If I go with him, that will leave you with no doctor.'

Kyla smiled. 'Logan's still on the island and he won't be long, I'm sure. Don't make the mistake of thinking that you're indispensable, Dr Walker,' she said cheerfully, her eyes sliding to Doug's taut features. 'We nurses are extremely versatile.'

His gaze followed hers and he frowned and checked Doug's pulse. 'How's the pain now? Any improvement?'

Doug nodded. 'Better,' he rasped, just as Evanna came back into the room.

'Air ambulance will be here in fifteen minutes,' she said in her calm, gentle voice. 'I've explained to the patients in the waiting room that there will be a delay until Logan gets back.'

Kyla looked up. 'Did you call him?'

'Yes. Mrs Taylor has a nasty laceration of her leg and she's very shaken up but nothing's broken. He's going to bring her back here to be sutured and I've said that one of us will spend some time in the home with her, discussing how to avoid falls.'

Kyla frowned as she reached for the phone. 'She ought to join your exercise class, Evanna. Did she trip over something?'

'Not sure. Janet just found her at the bottom of the stairs. It was fortunate that she didn't break anything or we'd be keeping the ambulance busy today.' Evanna glanced at her watch. 'If you don't need me here, I'll get started. I'm going to filter Logan's patients and see as many as I can for him.'

She left the room and Kyla handed Ethan the phone. 'You'll want to speak to the head of the coronary care unit at the Infirmary. His name's

Angus Marsh. He's a nice guy.' She walked over to Douglas. 'It's time we let your wife know what's going on. This is an Island, Doug. She'll see the air ambulance and pretty soon someone is going to tell her who the patient was. The first thing she'll do is worry and what will be going on in her head is going to be worse than the real thing. The second thing she'll do is kill me.'

As if to prove her point, the door flew open at that moment and Leslie hurried into the room.

'Who needs phones when there's the island grapevine?' Kyla breathed, stepping back from the couch and watching as Leslie lifted her hands to her cheeks.

'What have you been doing to yourself, Douglas Rory Fraser McDonald?'

Doug gave a feeble groan but there was no missing the affection in his eyes. 'What are you doing here, woman?'

'I was buying fish from Geoff on the quay and he told me he'd seen you looking really off colour and heading up this way.' Leslie stared at the ECG machine in horror and then turned to Kyla. 'Nurse MacNeil? What's going on?'

Kyla's gaze flickered to Ethan but he was on the phone, talking to the consultant at the hospital, arranging the transfer. 'Douglas has had some chest pain and it looks as though he might have had a heart attack,' she said gently. 'He's doing very well and there's certainly no need to panic. We're going to transfer him to the mainland just until they're happy with his condition. Just a precaution. The helicopter is going to be here in a minute.'

Leslie gave a soft gasp. 'You're going to the mainland? You've had a heart attack? And just when were you planning on telling me this, Doug? Next Christmas?'

'Stop fussing. Kyla was just about to ring you but they've been working flat out since I arrived.' Doug kept his eyes closed and his voice was thready. 'Go back and check on our Andrea. I'll call you from the hospital.'

'Andrea is fine. She's thirteen now. She can get

herself to school.' Leslie looked at Kyla, her face grey with shock and worry. 'Can I go with him?'

Kyla nodded. 'You should be able to but I'll have to check with the crew. Leslie, you look very pale. Sit down.' She quickly dragged a chair across the room and the other woman plopped onto it gratefully.

'I'll be fine in a minute,' she muttered, rubbing her hand across her forehead. 'It's just a bit of a shock, that's all.'

Ethan replaced the phone just as Evanna popped her head round the door again. 'The helicopter is here. The paramedics are bringing a stretcher in for you.'

'I've spoken to the hospital and they're expecting him.' Ethan checked Doug's observations again and then helped the paramedics move him onto the stretcher.

They loaded Doug into the helicopter, helped Leslie on board and then Ethan sprang up beside him in a lithe, athletic movement. 'How do I get back?'

Kyla grinned. 'If you're lucky, they bring you back. If you're unlucky, you swim. Don't worry, the water's quite warm at this time of the year. See you later, Dr Walker.'

She ducked out of range of the helicopter's blades and made her way back into the surgery. Walking into the crowded waiting room, she explained what had happened and quickly assessed who could see her instead of a doctor.

'Is Doug going to be all right?' Paula Stiles, who worked in the gift shop, asked the question that was on everyone's mind.

Patient confidentiality was a total nightmare, Kyla reflected as she gave as little information as possible while still providing the necessary reassurance.

Then she opened the door of her own room and switched on the computer. Interesting start to the day, she mused as she tapped a few keys and brought up her list for the morning. Not even nine o'clock and already she felt as though she'd done a day's work.

And she didn't want to think about how Ethan must feel. He'd travelled for most of the night to catch the first ferry and now she'd had to send him back to the mainland, and she knew from experience that he'd be lucky to make it back before lunch.

She hoped the new doctor had stamina because he was going to need it.

CHAPTER THREE

HER first patient was the headmistress from the local primary school, who had been hoping to see Logan and be back in time for the start of the school day.

'I'm sorry you've had a wait, Mrs Carne,' Kyla said, her tone apologetic as she reached for a pen. 'If it's your asthma that's bothering you, I could discuss it with you and then we could talk to Logan later.'

'It is my asthma.' Ann Carne put her bag on the floor and sat on the chair. 'I've been having problems on the sports field. Can you imagine that? I'm dealing with six-year-olds and I'm getting out of breath.'

'Six-year-olds are extremely energetic,' Kyla

said dryly. 'Don't underestimate the impact that can have on your breathing. I went to sports day last year and I was exhausted just watching. So what's happening? Are you using an inhaler before you exercise?'

'Sometimes.' Ann looked uncomfortable. 'I try to sneak off to the staffroom but it isn't always possible.'

'Why would you need to sneak?'

'I don't want the children knowing I have an inhaler.'

Kyla looked at her, trying to work out what the problem was so that she could tackle it in a sensitive way. 'Are you worried about them or you?'

'Both?' Ann gave a rueful smile. 'I hate admitting I'm ill and I don't want the children worrying that I'm going to collapse in front of them.'

'Would they think that?' Kyla frowned and tapped her pen on the desk. 'There are a couple of asthmatics in your school, as you well know. The children are used to seeing inhalers and spacers.'

'But not in their teachers.'

Judging that the situation was more about Ann than the pupils, Kyla sat back in her chair. 'It's nearly a year since you were diagnosed, Ann. How do you feel about it all now?'

There was a long silence and then Ann breathed out heavily. 'I still can't believe it's me,' she said finally. 'I mean, I'm fifty-two years of age. It's ridiculous! How can I suddenly develop asthma out of nowhere?'

'People do. It isn't about age. There are many other factors involved.'

'Well, I can't get used to the idea.'

'Is that why you don't use the inhaler?' Kyla's voice was gentle. 'If you don't use the drugs then you can't be ill?'

'How did you come to be so wise?' Ann gave a faint smile. 'I remember you when you were six years old, Kyla MacNeil. You brought a frog into my class and hid it in your desk.'

'I remember. It was my brother's frog. He was pretty annoyed with me.'

'And he came thundering in to steal it back.'

Ann sighed. 'I still think of myself as young, you know. I don't feel any different. It's only when I look in the mirror that I realise how many years have passed. And when my body starts letting me down.'

'Your body is still ready to work perfectly well if you give it the little bit of help it needs.' Kyla reached into her drawer for a leaflet. 'Read this. A bundle arrived last week and I think it's good. It talks about living with a condition rather than being ruled by it. You wouldn't dream of not using a toothbrush and toothpaste, would you? All part of body maintenance. Well, your inhalers are the same. Body maintenance.'

Ann took the leaflet and gave a thoughtful smile. 'Body maintenance. That's a nice idea, Kyla.'

'For the next two weeks, promise me you'll use your inhaler as we agreed. Then come and see me and we'll discuss how things are. But don't hide it from the children. We try and teach the children that it can become a normal part of life. Something they can live with. If they see you hiding it then it won't do much for their own acceptance of asthma.'

'I hadn't thought of that but you're right, of course.' Ann stood up and gave her a grateful smile. 'You've come a long way since you made a mess of your geography books, Kyla MacNeil. Can I ask how Doug is or will you tell me to mind my own business?'

'I don't think I'm ever going to be able to tell my old headmistress to mind her own business.' Kyla laughed. 'But the truth is that it's too soon for us to say.' The entire island had obviously noted the arrival of the helicopter. 'Our new doctor went with him. Hopefully we'll have good news when he arrives back. I'll remind Ben to pin a bulletin to the door of the pub.'

'You do that.' Ann gave a brisk nod. 'We all care, you know.'

'I do know,' Kyla said with a soft smile. 'That's why I choose to live on Glenmore, Mrs Carne. Have a good day, now. And don't let any of those little monsters bring frogs into the classroom.'

* * *

Ethan arrived back towards the end of her surgery, about an hour after her brother had returned from seeing Janet's mother.

Kyla showed him into his consulting room and together the three of them swiftly cleared the remaining patients in the waiting room while Evanna played the role of receptionist.

'Any house calls?' Logan stifled a yawn as they finally collapsed at the reception desk.

'Just the one. Helen McNair. Had some bad news from the hospital and wondered if you'd call.' Evanna picked up the book. 'I managed to persuade the rest of them to come to surgery this afternoon to save you going out again. I thought you'd need some time to show Dr Walker around.'

'You talked someone out of a house call?' Logan's drawl was tinged with humour. 'Evanna, consider yourself promoted, my angel. From now on you're officially our receptionist and my favourite woman.'

Kyla noticed the betraying pink of Evanna's cheeks and glanced towards her brother with sudden interest, but he'd picked up the latest copy of a medical journal and was flicking through the pages, apparently oblivious to the effect that his endearment had had on her friend.

Shaking her head with frustration, Kyla resisted the temptation to hit him over the head with a blunt object. Didn't the entire Island population praise Logan for his amazing sensitivity? Didn't everyone think her brother knew everything about everything and everyone?

Well, there were some things that he was totally dense about, Kyla thought wearily as she tucked a set of notes back into the cabinet. It had been almost a year since Catherine had died. Long enough. Sooner or later she was going to have to interfere.

Looking at the wistful expression in Evanna's kind eyes, Kyla decided that it might just be sooner. 'I had a visit from Ann Carne this morning.' Dragging her mind back to the job in hand, she handed a set of results to her brother.

'Did you, now?' Logan leaned back in his chair, his long legs stretched out in front of him. 'And how was our favourite headmistress?'

'Still in denial. If she doesn't learn to use those inhalers, she's going to find herself in trouble.'

Logan nodded thoughtfully. 'And did you speak to her about it?'

Kyla lifted an eyebrow. 'What am I—stupid?'

'You want me to answer that?'

'Don't start, you two,' Evanna said hastily, sending an apologetic glance towards Ethan. 'You mustn't mind them. It's just brother-sister stuff. They're always the same. They bicker and needle. You get used to it after a time. They adore each other really.'

There was no answering smile on Ethan's face and Kyla frowned slightly as she noticed the grim set of his mouth and the tension in his broad shoulders. Oops, she thought to herself. Trouble there. There was a bleakness and a shadow in his eyes that made her wonder and want to ask questions. Did he object to humour in the workplace? Surely not.

She caught Logan's eye and he shot her a warning look. 'Mind your own business,' he murmured softly in Gaelic, and she smiled and replied in the same tongue.

'Perhaps I'm wondering whether to make him my business.'

Logan rolled his eyes and stood up, switching to English. 'Women. I'll never understand them.'

'Well, that's perfectly obvious,' Kyla muttered, her eyes sliding to Evanna. 'But don't give up trying. Believe me, you need the practice.'

'I'm practising on my daughter. Talking of which, if we've finished here I'm going to spend an hour with the girl in my life who should be just about waking up from her nap and ready to dress herself in her lunch. Ethan, I'd invite you to join us but you'd end up covered in puréed vegetables. Take some time to settle in. My sister will show you the cottage we've arranged for you. I hope it suits. It's only a short drive from here. If you need anything, you've only to ask.'

Kyla watched as some of the wariness left Ethan's handsome face. 'Do you want me to do the house call so you can spend more time with the baby?'

'No need.' Logan shook his head. 'I'll take her with me. Helen McNair has been asking to see her.'

Kyla gave a soft smile. 'That's a clever idea, Logan MacNeil. Give her something else to focus on.'

'She's had a hard time lately. It will be good to spend some time with her. And she makes the best chocolate cake on the island.' Logan strode across the reception area towards the door that separated the surgery from his house.

Kyla turned to Ethan with a smile. 'Are you ready for another trip in my car?'

'That was an exciting morning.' Ethan unravelled himself from the car and followed Kyla down a path that led towards a pair of cottages. The sea stretched ahead of them and he breathed in deeply, enjoying the cool, salty breeze and the freshness of the air. 'Is it always like that?'

'Sometimes.' She pushed open a gate and held it while he followed her through. 'It's often all or nothing. You were good.'

'Was it a test?'

'No. But if it had been, you would have passed.' She let the gate swing shut and tilted her head to one side as she studied him. 'Don't be angry with me. Working on this island isn't for everyone. We see everything here, and we're the first line of defence. Does that worry you?'

'No.' What worried him was the hot flare of lust he felt whenever he looked at her. Gritting his teeth, he concentrated on the view of the bay. 'It's spectacular. Who lives here usually?'

'Holiday let. The cottage is usually rented out for the whole of the summer season but Nick Hillier who owns it had a bad experience last year.' Kyla fumbled for the keys and opened the front door. 'A group from London had a bit of a wild party and left the place wrecked. So he decided that this summer he'd let it to the locum doctor. He's assuming that, with all those letters after your name, you'll know how to behave yourself.'

'I'll do my best.' Ethan strolled into the cottage behind her, trying to ignore her delicious scent and the incredible shine of her honey-blonde hair. 'Who's Nick Hillier?'

'Our policeman. I went to school with him. He used to tie my plaits together.'

For some reason that he couldn't identify, this piece of news simply racked up the tension inside him and Ethan drew in a breath and rolled his shoulders. He needed a swim. A run. Anything to drive the unwanted thoughts and images from his head.

He watched as she threw open doors and windows, letting in light and air. She was obviously an outdoor sort of person. 'Did you go to school with everyone on the island?'

'Not everyone, but most of the people of

around my age who were born here. It's a small community. Mind you, that can be a disadvantage. I sometimes think Ann Carne still sees me as the little horror who led the strike against school dinners.' She turned and smiled and he felt a vicious kick of lust deep inside him.

Her pretty smile faded and was replaced by something entirely different as they stared at each other.

Back off, Ethan, he warned himself grimly. Not now. *And not this woman.*

That wasn't why he was there.

'You led a strike against school dinners?' He saw from the slightly questioning look in her eyes that she'd picked up on the rough tone of his voice.

'I was a fussy eater. I protested loudly about everything they put in front of me and I expected everyone else to protest, too. I told all the other children to fold their arms and refuse to eat until they produced something decent.'

He could imagine her doing it. Imagine her

with those sapphire-blue eyes flashing and that chin lifted in defiance. 'And how old were you?'

'Five.' She smiled without a trace of apology. 'My mother said she'd never been so embarrassed. They called her down to the school. I was given such a talking-to.'

Ethan found himself smiling, too. 'And did you eat your dinner after that?'

'No. I used to scrape it into my napkin and then hide the evidence.'

'And they never found out?'

'Sadly, they did.' Kyla opened a door and walked ahead of him into a beautiful glass-fronted living room, her feet echoing on the pale wooden floor. 'But only because I was stupid enough to slide it into Miss Carne's handbag on one occasion. I think it was lasagne or something really sloppy. Vile. I'm surprised I wasn't expelled. After that, they watched me eat.'

'I don't blame them.' He glanced around him in surprise. 'This is nice.'

'You should have seen it two years ago.

Complete wreck. It had been lived in by the same man for about ninety years. After he bought it, Nick spent every weekend doing it up. We all helped.' She walked over to the window and stared out across the sea. 'He was lucky to get it. There was a lot of competition because this is one of the best spots on the island.'

'So why didn't you try and buy it?'

'I didn't need to.' She turned to look at him, amusement in her eyes. 'I own the place next door. You might want to remember that before you run naked into the waves for your morning swim, Dr Walker. Or are you southerners too wimpy to take a plunge into the Atlantic?'

Was she challenging him? He held her gaze with his own. 'I swim well.'

Her eyes slid to his shoulders, as if she were assessing the truth of his quiet statement and suddenly the tension in the air snapped as tight as a bow and Ethan felt something dangerous stir inside him.

'So this place is mine for the duration of my

stay?' His voice was hoarse and he cursed himself. *Could she feel it, too?* Was she aware of the sudden change in the atmosphere?

'It's yours for as long as you want it. When you leave it will be winter and no one but the locals brave this island come November.' She watched him for a moment and then walked over to the French doors, her movements as smooth and graceful as those of a dancer. But then she lifted a hand to touch a switch and he saw that her fingers were shaking. 'Flick this to the right and the doors open. The garden leads down to the beach. Just make sure you close the doors if there's a storm or you'll be sweeping the sand from your living room for weeks.'

'Storm?' Ethan fixed his gaze on the perfect blue sky. *He needed to stay away from her.* Far, far away. 'Jim, the ferryman, mentioned storms. It's pretty calm today. Hard to imagine the place in a storm.'

'You won't have to imagine it because you're going to see it soon enough.' Kyla gave a soft laugh. 'I hope you like your weather wild, Dr Walker, and I hope you're not afraid of storms. Because anything you've seen up until now will be nothing compared to this island in the grip of a seething temper.'

'I don't scare easily.' He turned, unable to be in the same room and not look at her. 'How about you, Kyla MacNeil? Do you scare easily? Do you take risks?' He was playing with fire. *Testing her.* He saw from the fierce glint in her blue eyes that she knew it.

'Life is there to be lived to the full. I was born on this island and it's part of who I am. Nothing about it frightens me. Not the storms. Not the isolation.' *And not you,* her eyes said, and he felt a flicker of envy.

What would it be like, Ethan wondered bleakly, to be so sure of everything? To live somewhere that felt like home?

The letter was still in his pocket and suddenly he wanted to read it again. *To try and understand.*

'I need to unpack and take a shower.' His tone

was harsher than he'd intended and he saw the faint frown of confusion in her eyes. For a brief moment he wanted to take her arm and apologise, and the impulse surprised him as much as it would have surprised all of the people who knew him because he wasn't exactly known for gentleness.

You don't have a heart, Ethan.

And then he backed off, remembering that he wasn't in a position to explain anything.

He needed time.

There were things he needed to find out.

Kyla closed the front door behind her and jumped over the tiny hedge that separated the two cottages.

As she let herself into the cottage that she'd converted with the help of her brother and her friends, she considered the powerful chemistry between Ethan and herself. It was there. Pointless to deny it. And yet she sensed that the connection angered him.

He didn't want to feel it.

Kyla frowned as she flicked on the kettle. And what about her? What did she want?

She'd become so used to leading her own life she hadn't given any thought to the possibility that things might change.

He wasn't going to stay, she told herself firmly as she made herself a mug of tea and took it out onto the deck that overlooked the beach. Whatever they shared would be short-term because she would never leave the island.

'Nurse MacNeil! Kyla!'

She glanced up as she heard her name being called from the beach. Deciding that perhaps the prospect of leaving the island had possibilities after all, she gave a sigh and walked down to the end of her garden, still nursing the mug. At least in inner-city London she might get to drink her tea in peace. 'Fraser Price. What are you doing on the beach in the middle of a school day?'

Probably bunking off, the way she had as a child.

'Don't tell Miss Carne,' the boy begged,

breathless as he struggled in bare feet through the soft sand. 'She thinks I'm ill.'

'And you're not?' Reminding herself that she was a grown-up now and supposed to set standards, Kyla looked suitably stern. 'You should be at school. Education is important. Pretending to be ill isn't a good idea, Fraser.' She almost laughed as she listened to herself. *How many times had she sneaked off to play on the beach?*

'It was the only thing I could think of. And I needed to stay at home.'

'Why did you need to stay at home?'

'To look after Mum.' Suddenly he looked doubtful and unsure. 'She wasn't making sense this morning and I didn't want to leave her. I had a bad feeling.'

'What sort of bad feeling?' Kyla was alert now. 'Is it her diabetes? What do you mean, she wasn't making sense? Is something the matter with your mum?'

'I dunno. She just seemed…different.' He gave a shake of his head and then shrugged.

'She'd kill me if she knew I was here. I bunked off last week to take the boat out and she really did her nut. Don't say I was here. Couldn't you just call in on her? You know, like by accident?'

'Fraser, I don't call on anyone by accident.' Amusement gave way to concern as Kyla saw the look on his face. 'OK. OK.' She lifted a hand. 'Today I'll find a reason to call on your mum by accident.'

'Really?' He breathed an audible sigh of relief. 'That's great. Can the accident be right now?'

Banishing hopes of lunch, Kyla nodded. 'Just let me lock up here and get my car. I'll meet you back at your house. You can let me in. And, Fraser, about your mum…' She caught his arm. 'Can you describe how she looked? How was she different?'

'She was a funny colour. And her hands were shaking when she gave me breakfast. You won't tell on me?' He looked at her anxiously. 'I said I felt sick and needed a walk in the fresh air.'

Kyla thought of all the sins she'd committed at

school. Didn't everyone need a little latitude? 'I
won't tell. Off you go. I'll be there in five minutes.'

'What will you say?'

'I don't know, but I'll think of something,'
Kyla said firmly, giving him a gentle push and
turning back to her cottage. She noticed Ethan
standing in his garden and had a sudden inspi-
ration. 'Dr Walker!'

He turned and she gave an apologetic shrug.
'How badly did you want a shave and a shower?
If you're not that tired, I need to enlist your help
again. I think I might need a doctor.'

CHAPTER FOUR

'AISLA PRICE is a single mother.' Kyla snapped on her seat belt and pressed her foot to the accelerator. 'She moved to the island when Fraser was a baby because she thought it would be a good place to bring up a child. She has a small knitting business that she runs over the internet. Pretty successfully, I believe. She makes really pretty jumpers covered in bits of lace and beads and things like that. They live in a house right by the water.'

Ethan looked at her. 'And she has diabetes?'

'Yes. But her diabetes is very well controlled so it shouldn't be that.' Kyla frowned as she changed gear and flicked the indicator. 'But

Fraser obviously thinks there's a problem so we'd better check it out. It might be nothing.'

'She hasn't asked you to call? You're making an impromptu visit?' Ethan tried to imagine something similar happening in London and failed. But in London a child wouldn't run across a beach to bang on the community nurse's door.

'That's right. An impromptu visit.' She stopped the car outside a row of whitewashed cottages and yanked on the handbrake. 'We're here.'

Ethan looked at her in disbelief. 'What on earth are you planning to say? You're going to bang on her door and say that her little boy thought she looked pale at breakfast?'

'No. That's why I'm taking you along.' She smiled and reached for her bag. 'You're the new doctor and I'm introducing you. She'll be your patient after all. You may as well meet each other.'

Wondering why he was on a wild-goose chase when he could be in the shower, Ethan slammed the car door and followed her towards the house.

The front door opened and it took less than a second for him to register the raw panic in Fraser's eyes.

'You have to come quickly! She's on the floor,' he said urgently, reaching out a hand and virtually dragging Kyla inside. 'And I can't get her to wake up properly. She's sort of moaning and trying to hit me.'

Ethan sprinted past him into the house, leaving Kyla to deal with the panicked child.

The woman was slumped on the floor of the kitchen, the remains of a cup of coffee spread over the quarry tiles. With a soft curse he dropped into a crouch and checked her pulse.

'Has she died?' The small voice came from behind him and Ethan turned.

'She's not dead. Fraser…' He kept his voice calm and steady so as not to frighten the child further. 'I need my bag from Kyla's car. Do you think you could fetch it for me? It's on the back seat.'

The little boy nodded and sprinted out of the

room while Kyla dropped to her knees beside him. 'Aisla?'

The woman gave a groan and her eyes fluttered open and then closed again as she muttered something incoherent.

'Sugar,' Ethan instructed, glancing around him. 'Would you know where to find it?'

'Not a clue.' Kyla sprang to her feet and started opening cupboards. 'Come on, Aisla, where do you keep your sugar?' She rummaged through packets and bottles. 'Soy sauce, pasta, turmeric, honey. Harissa paste—what on earth is Harissa paste? Gosh, do people really use all this stuff? No wonder cooking confuses me.'

'Hurry up, Kyla,' Ethan growled, and she yanked open a few more cupboards.

'Lucozade. That will do.' She lifted it down just as Fraser ran back into the room with Ethan's bag. 'Can we get her to drink, do you think, or is she past that?'

'We should be able to manage it.' Ethan scooped the woman up and Kyla held the glass to her lips.

'Aisla.' Her voice was firm. 'You need to drink this.'

Aisla murmured something incoherent and tried to push them away, but Kyla held the glass and eventually she took a few sips.

'More,' Kyla urged. 'You're doing well, Aisla. Just a bit more.'

The woman drank properly and Kyla glanced towards Fraser, who was standing rigid, a look of horror on his face. 'She's going to be fine, sweetheart. Do you have any biscuits in the house?'

Fraser looked at her and some of the tension left his little body. 'Of course.' A flicker of a smile appeared. 'Chocolate ones. Really yummy. But I'm only allowed them on special occasions.'

'This is a special occasion,' Kyla assured him hastily. 'And a glass of milk, please.'

'Can you manage here for a second?' Ethan reached for his bag. 'I want to check her blood sugar.'

'She's coming round,' Kyla murmured. 'Why would she have gone hypo? Fraser, what did your mum do this morning? Anything different to usual?'

'She was late getting up.' Fraser was on a chair, reaching for a tin. 'I had to shake her. Why are you pricking her finger?'

'We're trying to find out the level of sugar in her blood.' Ethan read the result and nodded. 'Well that's your culprit. It's less than three. Perhaps she overdid the insulin. Fraser, has your mum done any exercise this morning?'

Handing the tin to Kyla, Fraser shook his head. 'No. But she went for a run on the beach last night. I know because I took my book down and sat while she ran up and down the beach. Is that why she's been acting funny?'

'I don't know, but I intend to find out. I'm going to take a blood sample and send it off,' Ethan told Kyla, reaching for a blood bottle. 'I want a more accurate blood glucose level.'

By the time he'd taken the sample and labelled the bottle, Kyla had fed Aisla several chocolate biscuits and she was rapidly recovering.

'I can't believe I let that happen,' she groaned, struggling to her feet with Ethan's help. 'It was such a sunny evening yesterday I just couldn't resist a trip to the beach. And then when I got there I thought I'd do some exercise.' I was going to eat as soon as I got in but Fraser's uncle rang and then I sort of lost track and just went to bed. I'm so sorry. How did you find me?'

Ethan opened his mouth to give the honest answer, but Kyla jumped in. 'We were passing,' she said quickly. 'I wanted to introduce you to Dr Walker.'

'Well, this isn't the way I would have chosen to meet you,' Aisla said with a weary smile, 'but thanks. I owe you both. If you hadn't called, goodness knows what would have happened.'

Ethan saw Kyla glance towards Fraser. Saw her smile of reassurance and praise.

Aisla followed that look. 'Fraser?' Her voice was gentle. 'Are you all right? Didn't you say something about feeling sick?'

'I'm feeling a lot better now,' he said firmly. 'Ever since I had that fresh air on the beach.'

'Fresh air can be a miracle-worker,' Kyla said blithely, and Fraser breathed an audible sigh of relief.

'I can't believe that this is an average working day. Do you ever get any time off for good behaviour?' Ethan slid into the car beside her and Kyla smiled.

'The nature of this island is that we're permanently on call. But it isn't usually this bad, honestly. And now you definitely deserve some time off. I'll drop you home on my way to the clinic. But have dinner with Logan and me tonight. It's the least we can do, having pushed you straight into the deep end.' She saw his expression change. Saw surprise flicker in the depths of his dark, dangerous eyes.

'You eat dinner with your brother?'

'Of course,' Kyla said comfortably. 'We're family.'

'But not all families eat together and socialise.'

'Well, we do. Usually several times a week. Is that so strange?' Kyla looked at him in confusion, wondering why that would seem odd to him. As far as she was concerned, it was so normal it wasn't even worth commenting on. 'I love seeing my niece and usually one of my aunts or cousins are there. It'll probably be a pretty noisy evening but it will be nice for you to meet some of the islanders. One of my aunts runs the café on the quay and another has a knitwear boutique in Glenmore village. Two of my other cousins are fisherman. They also man the lifeboat when it's necessary.'

'What about your parents?'

'They moved over to the mainland two months ago to be with my other aunt. My uncle died and she needs help on the farm, so my parents moved in and took over. But we still get together all the time.'

'You're a close family.'

'Are we?' She frowned and then gave a shrug.

'A pretty normal family, I would have said. We have our rows and disagreements and we're pretty noisy but, yes, we like each other's company and we're in and out of each other's lives. Why wouldn't we be? What about you? Are you a big family? Brothers? Sisters?' She saw the immediate change in him. His dark eyes were blank. Shuttered—as if something had slammed closed inside him.

'Just me.' His tone was cool and his eyes slid away from hers. 'My parents divorced when I was eight and my father's second marriage didn't last long either.'

'Oh.' Kyla tried to imagine not having her family round her and failed. Maybe that explained why he was reserved and slightly aloof. 'That must have been pretty tough on you.'

'On the contrary, it was a relief from the interminable rows. And it made me independent.' He frowned, as if he hadn't even considered the subject before. 'I had a very free and easy childhood because everyone was too busy fighting to be remotely interested in what I was doing. From my point of view, it was a good thing.'

A good thing? It didn't sound like a good thing to Kyla. 'But one of the joys of childhood is being fussed over. Knowing that someone cares. It's about loving and being loved.' Puzzled by his observation, she lifted her eyes to his and saw the faint gleam of mockery there.

'Perhaps it depends what sort of person you are. Don't feel sorry for me, Kyla,' he advised in a soft drawl. 'I've never been touchy-feely. I don't need hugs.'

'Everyone needs hugs.' *Even people like him.* He was tough and aloof. Independent.

'I prefer to handle my problems myself. In private.'

Kyla laughed. 'Actually, so would I sometimes. But it's virtually impossible if you live here. On Glenmore, people not only know everything about your problems, they all think they know the best way of solving them. And they let you know. Loudly and quite often in the pub when you're trying to have a quiet drink. Come for supper tonight. Really. It will be a gentle introduction to the realities of living on an island. Sort of sanitised nosiness.'

Her humorous observation drew a smile from him. 'I thought you didn't cook.'

'I don't. But luckily for you, Evanna does. Extremely well. And tonight it's seafood. You should come, it will be fun. If the weather holds, we'll eat in Logan's garden and no doubt my niece will create havoc.' She tried to keep her voice light. *Tried not to stare.* His hair was rumpled and his jaw was dark with stubble, but she'd never seen a more attractive man in her life.

'The baby will be there?'

Kyla dragged her eyes away from her surreptitious study of his mouth. 'Well, she's not really a baby any more. More of a toddler. Life has grown a great deal more complicated for everyone since she started crawling. But, yes, she'll be there.' She noticed the sudden tension in his shoulders. 'Is that a problem?'

'Why would it be a problem?'

'I don't know.' But she sensed something. 'You just seem…' There was something in his cool gaze that she found intimidating and she broke off and gave a small shrug. If he came from such a small, fractured family then he probably just wasn't used to children. 'Nothing. Anyway, you're welcome if you want to join us. I can give you a lift.' Her heart was pounding hard against her chest and she wondered what it was about him that had such a powerful effect on her.

'I think my relationship with your car has reached its conclusion,' he drawled with a sardonic lift of his eyebrow. 'My own car is arriving this afternoon. I'll give you a lift.'

'Does that mean you're coming?'

His hesitation was fractional, but it was there. 'Yes. If you're sure your brother won't mind.'

'The more, the merrier.' Her heart gave a little skip and she lectured herself fiercely.

She shouldn't care whether he was coming or not. This was *not* a man to get involved with. There were too many shadows around his eyes. And the little he'd revealed about himself hinted at an extremely scarred childhood. And any man who didn't need hugs was never going to suit her. 'Can you pick me up at six? We eat early because Logan puts Kirsty down around seven o'clock and I like to have some time with her.'

He sat for a moment without moving. 'How does he manage?'

'With the baby? Very well. Logan's a brilliant father. Fun, loving and amazingly hands-on considering the job he does.' Kyla shrugged. 'He has to have help, of course, otherwise he wouldn't be able to work. My aunts work out a rota, and I help when I can. My cousins muck in and he's employed a few girls from the village, but that hasn't really worked out.'

'Why? Weren't they competent?'

'Perfectly competent. But they all had

serious designs on my brother,' Kyla said in a dry voice. 'It would seem as though there's nothing more appealing to a single woman than a sexy doctor with a baby. Amy Foster is helping at the moment and we're all laying bets on how long it takes her to make a pass at Logan.'

'What about Evanna? She mentioned helping out.'

Kyla gave a soft smile. 'Evanna adores the baby.'

'And I suppose she's not likely to fall for your brother.'

Kyla laughed, wondering what it was about men that made them so unobservant. 'Evanna's been in love with my brother all her life. One day I'm hoping he'll wake up and notice. Otherwise I just might have to interfere and that won't be a pretty sight.' She pulled up outside the cottages and saw him staring out to sea, his handsome face an expressionless mask. 'You're very difficult to read, do you know that?'

He turned his head. 'Why would you want to read me?'

'It's easier to deal with people if you understand them.'

A faint smile played around his firm mouth. 'I have no particular desire to be understood,' he said softly, 'so you can relax.'

'Is it too isolated from civilisation for you here? Do you hate it?' For a long moment he didn't reply and she was starting to wonder whether he'd even heard her question when he turned his head away and stared at the sea once more.

'I don't hate it.'

What sort of an answer was that? He was a man who revealed nothing about his thoughts or feelings, she thought with mounting frustration as she switched off the engine. 'Thanks for helping me with Aisla. I'll see you at six, Dr Walker. Enjoy your shower.'

Ethan let himself into the cottage, changed into his running gear and let himself out of the back of the house. He needed a shower, a shave and a rest, but none of those options tempted him. He didn't want what he needed.

What he wanted was to run. Fast.

The conversation with Kyla had disturbed him and he didn't understand why.

All he knew what that he intended to drive out the thoughts from his head with hard exercise.

Despite the sunshine, a strong wind gusted, but Ethan didn't even notice, his expression grim and intent as he jogged to the end of the garden and down onto the beach.

As soon as his feet hit the sand he picked up speed, his long, powerful legs covering the ground in rhythmic, pounding strides as he pushing his body to its limits. His arms and legs pumped, his heart thumped and the sweat prickled between his shoulder blades, but still he ran, lengthening his stride until his pace would have been the envy of the wind. Still he pushed himself, giving himself no slack.

He ran until the sand ended and the cliff path

rose upwards. He hit the slope with a fierce determination, maintaining his punishing speed through a mixture of willpower and physical fitness, his lungs and his muscles screaming a protest that he ignored.

He felt the rapid pumping of his heart as it responded to the demands of physical exertion, felt his body burn as his arms and legs pounded the earth. Felt his brain empty of everything except the need to focus on the physical task in hand.

Run, Ethan. Run.

And if he ran fast enough and hard enough, perhaps none of it would hurt any more.

Kyla stood at the bedroom window and watched.

Ethan ran like a professional athlete.

Or a man with the devil at his heels.

Even from this distance she could sense the grim determination that drove his long stride. She could almost feel the power and force of his body as he took on the elements and pushed himself with almost superhuman effort.

Kyla stared, unable to look away, captivated by the unexpected display of masculinity.

She'd only popped into the house to collect something for her afternoon clinic but then she'd happened to glance out of the window. She'd begun watching out of concern, sure that such physical exertion would cause an injury and then her gaze had turned almost greedy as she realised exactly what she was watching.

A male in his prime, at the peak of physical fitness.

This was no city boy out for a guilt-driven exercise session. This was a man who regularly pushed his body to the limit.

He ran with rhythm and surprising grace, drawing on all the strength and power of his body to meet the challenge he'd set himself.

She couldn't see his face and yet she knew that his expression would have been set and determined. Focussed. Bleak?

Sensing that his run was more than a desire to

raise his pulse rate, Kyla turned away, giving him the privacy he so clearly craved, her curiosity well and truly piqued. Her own body suddenly stirred to an uncomfortable degree.

Who was he?

His cool indifference and aloof approach to life was completely alien to her.

Who was this man who held himself slightly apart from others? And why did he affect her so strongly?

She'd spent too long cooped up on an island with people she knew too well, that was why.

Ethan Walker was a stranger. And when you lived with people who were entirely familiar, strangers were always interesting.

It was no more than that.

She gave herself a mental shake and reminded herself that she had less than ten minutes to get back to the surgery or she'd have Logan on her back.

* * *

Logan's house was attached to the surgery and opened onto a huge garden crowded with mature apple trees.

Fresh from the shower after a busy clinic, Kyla pushed open the back gate and walked straight into the kitchen without knocking.

'Oh!' Evanna was standing in front of the range, stirring something in a pot. Her dark hair was caught up in a ponytail, her cheeks were pink from the heat and she was wearing a loose white dress that was summery and pretty. 'You're early. Can you pass me the coriander, please?'

'Coriander?' Kyla glanced along the work surface in confusion. 'Is that this green, weedy-looking stuff?' She picked it up, sniffed and handed it to Evanna. 'If we're early, you can blame Ethan's car. You should see it. All black and very growly. Very high testosterone rating.' She peered over Evanna's shoulder into the pot. 'Is that our dinner? It looks nice, but nothing like barbecued seafood. Did you lose the recipe?'

'It's chicken soup, and it's for Kirsty who hasn't woken up yet from her nap. Logan is hopeless with routine. He keeps waking her up for a cuddle.' Evanna swiftly chopped the coriander, sprinkled it on the soup and glanced at her friend, a curious look in her eyes. 'So I notice you're calling the new doctor Ethan now? Getting friendly, are you?'

Kyla grinned. 'No. Not yet. But I could probably be persuaded. You should have seen him running along the beach earlier. I thought my heart was going to stop. What a body! Not that you notice things like that.'

'I'm not blind, Kyla,' Evanna said mildly as she stirred the soup slowly. 'I do know a handsome man when I see one, and Ethan is certainly very good looking.'

'But?' Kyla leaned forward and dipped a spoon in the soup, tasting it cautiously. 'There's a definite "but" coming. This soup is good. Can I take some for lunch tomorrow?'

'There's more to a man than looks, Kyla.'

Evanna gently slapped the back of her hand. 'Leave the soup alone. It's for Kirsty.'

'I'm the royal taster. And there's plenty more to Ethan than looks.'

Evanna frowned. 'That's what worries me. There are dark corners there. And mystery.'

'Dark corners? Mystery?' Kyla dropped the spoon in the sink, laughing to hide the effect that Evanna's words had had on her. 'You've been reading too many Celtic legends. Your imagination is in sprint mode. Spotted any fire-breathing dragons on your rounds?'

Evanna didn't smile. 'You can laugh, but I'm right. That man has secrets, Kyla.'

Kyla felt cold fingers of unease stroke her nerve endings. 'What sort of secrets?'

'If I knew that, they wouldn't be secrets, would they? But I don't think they're good ones.' Evanna stopped stirring and her pretty face was serious. 'There's something about him,' she said softly, glancing over her shoulder to check that they were on their own. 'Can't you feel it? A hardness. He's tough—a bit intimidating. I don't know…' She gave a shrug, obviously wishing she'd never said anything. 'Something's happened in his life, I'm sure of it. Something that he's living with every day of his life. He has issues.'

'Well, things have happened in our lives, too,' Kyla reminded her, trying to shake off the black, threatening cloud that hovered over her happiness, 'and we're living with them. We all have issues, Evanna.'

'That's true. Just be careful, that's all. I don't want to see you hurt by a man.'

'Wouldn't be the first time.'

Her friend looked at her and her expression softened. 'You haven't fallen for anyone since that rat, Mike Robinson, hoisted his sails and left for the mainland. It's time you found someone. I'm just not sure it should be Ethan. Is there something going on there or is it just wishful imagining on your part?'

'I'm not imagining the chemistry. I keep

thinking we're going to burn the cottage down every time we look at each other.' Kyla chewed her lip thoughtfully. 'I just have a feeling he isn't very pleased about it. He's fighting it.'

'Probably because he knows he's only here for the summer,' Evanna said briskly. 'Thank goodness one of you is sensible.'

'Well, it isn't me,' Kyla said lightly. 'You know I always pick the unsuitable. And what about you? Talking of issues, you're wearing a white dress to feed my niece chicken soup. A strange choice from where I'm standing, knowing what I do about Kirsty's aim. You're going to have serious stain issues.'

Evanna's colour deepened. 'I happen to like this dress.'

'So you should. It suits you. It's nice to see you in something other than jeans.' Kyla opened the drawer, fished out a spoon and dipped it into the soup. 'My brother will probably like it, too. Which, I'm guessing, was the intention.'

Evanna gave a wry smile. 'Your brother wouldn't notice me if I stripped naked in front of him and danced a tango.'

Kyla tasted the soup again. 'I've come to the sad conclusion that my brother is obviously thick. One day I'm going to tease him about it. But not before I've eaten his seafood. My stomach always comes before sibling conflict.'

'You mustn't mention it.' Evanna gave a faint frown. 'And to call him thick is just ridiculous when you know just how clever he is. It's just that he can only think of Catherine. And that's normal, of course,' she added hastily, emptying the soup into a blender and securing the lid. 'She was his wife. He loved her.'

Kyla waited for the noise of the blender to cease before she spoke. 'Yes, I think he did. But that doesn't mean he can't love again.'

Evanna's eyes met hers. 'It isn't going to happen, Kyla. Please stop talking about it.'

Kyla leaned forward and gave her friend a

hug. 'Give him time. Be patient.' She glanced up as Ethan strolled into the room and suddenly found herself unable to breathe.

'Logan has the barbecue going.' His voice was a smooth, cultured drawl. 'He wants to know what the pair of you are doing in here.'

'We're hugging. As friends should. Our Dr Walker isn't much of a hugger,' Kyla drawled, releasing Evanna and trying not to stare at Ethan. But it was hard to look away.

On the short car journey from their cottages, she hadn't had a chance to look at him, but she saw now that he'd showered and shaved and changed into a pair of black jeans and a casual shirt that clung to the muscles of his shoulders. Kyla felt her stomach flip and suddenly discovered that her fingers were shaking. She turned, dropped the spoon into the sink to hide her burning cheeks and gave herself a sharp talking-to. Evanna was right. She knew perfectly well that Ethan was complicated. But he was the only man who had ever made her want to sit down in case her legs gave way. It was pretty hard to ignore that degree of chemistry.

'We'll just get the prawns out of the fridge,' she mumbled, crossing the kitchen and tugging open the door. *Maybe cold air would help.* Plates of fresh seafood confronted her and she lifted them out and handed them to Ethan. 'Take these out. We'll follow with the salad.'

'You go out, Kyla.' Evanna poured some of the liquid soup into a bowl. 'I'll fetch Kirsty and join you in the garden.'

Logan and Ethan immediately started talking about what had happened with Aisla, and Kyla stared at the pile of uncooked food with a distinct lack of enthusiasm.

'Logan, could you cook and then talk? If someone doesn't feed me soon, my blood sugar will do something dramatic,' she said in a conversational tone, and her brother lifted an eyebrow in mockery.

'Is there something wrong with your arms?

What's stopping you putting food on the barbecue?'

'Possibly the memory of the stomachache I gave everyone last time I cooked.'

'Good point.' Logan grinned and she gave him a gentle push.

'Start cooking or none of us will be eating before midnight. Aisla is fine. And she's Ethan's patient now.'

'She's coming to see me at the surgery so that I can check her properly and we can talk. I'll cook.' Ethan stepped forward and picked up the plate. Soon he was placing food on the barbecue with swift efficiency and Kyla watched in admiration.

'You cook?'

He sent her an easy smile that had her heart racing. 'When I have time, I cook.'

Evanna was wrong, Kyla thought to herself, relaxing slightly. He didn't have demons. He was just naturally reserved. And here, in their garden, she could see him unwind.

Her theory lasted for as long as it took Kirsty

to lift the baby out of her crib and bring her downstairs.

'You have to stop letting her sleep so late, Logan,' Evanna scolded gently as she cuddled the wriggling toddler against her body. 'She needs a routine.'

'So do I,' Logan said dryly, snapping the top off a bottle of beer. 'Would someone mind telling our patients? I need a regular bedtime and regular meals. I can't function like this. It gives me indigestion.'

'I'm serious, Logan,' Evanna said. 'She's really hard to settle in the evenings because she doesn't know whether she's supposed to be awake or asleep.'

Logan sighed and reached out his arms for his daughter. 'Routine is overrated,' he said roughly, as he buried his face in the little girl's blonde curls. 'If she goes to bed early then there are some nights when I don't see her, and I don't want that. I need cuddles.'

Kyla's heart shifted as she saw the two of them

together and suddenly she found she had a lump in her throat. *He's a good father,* she thought to herself, and she knew from the soft expression in her friend's eyes that Evanna was thinking the same thing.

Then she looked at Ethan and something in his eyes caught her attention.

She saw shock, pain and desolation so huge that it almost hurt to watch.

And he was staring at the baby.

'I offered her some of my home-made soup,' Evanna was saying as she pulled faces at the little girl, drawing smiles of delight, 'but she wasn't interested.'

Had no one else noticed? Kyla wondered as she moved instinctively towards Ethan. Had no one else noticed the grim set of his mouth or the fact that his entire body was unnaturally still? It was as if he were afraid to move.

Did he hate babies? Had he lost a baby? What could possibly have happened in his life to trigger that sort of reaction?

Her mind sifted through options and came up
with nothing concrete.

Perhaps she was just being dramatic. He was
single after all. It was perfectly possible that he
just didn't like babies.

'She doesn't need soup, she needs attention.
Give your daddy a cuddle,' Logan drawled in a
soft voice, and the little girl gurgled with delight
and lifted her hand to pull his hair.

'Ow—you have got to stop doing that, sweet
pea, or Daddy is going to be bald and that is not
a "good look", as your Aunty Kyla would say.'
Logan wrapped his daughter's tiny fist in his
hand and planted a noisy kiss on her cheek.
'Pull someone else's hair. Kyla has plenty.'

'Ethan?' Kyla moved over to Ethan's side and
touched his arm. 'Are you all right?'

It was a moment before he even noticed she
was there. 'Of course.' His voice was flat. 'Why
wouldn't I be?'

'I don't know. You just seem—'

'Tired,' he supplied, his gaze cool as he turned

to look at her. 'It's been a long day and it was a long night before that. I probably should have made my excuses and had an early night instead of accepting the invitation.'

Was that what was wrong? He was tired?

Kyla glanced towards her niece and then back at him, searching for clues. She wanted to ask a question but she had no idea which words would lead her to the right answer. Why would the sight of a strange baby affect him so badly? It didn't make sense. 'She's sweet, isn't she?'

There was a long silence and Ethan's knuckles were white as he gripped the bottle of beer. 'I don't know much about babies,' he said hoarsely, lifting the bottle to his lips and drinking deeply, 'but I'm sure she's very sweet.'

He was a loner, Kyla reminded herself. A man who clearly had no experience of family. It was perfectly natural that he wouldn't be comfortable with babies. But somehow none of her reasoning made her feel better and Evanna's words of warning rang in her head.

'I had a call from the Infirmary on the mainland,' Logan said, strolling across to them. 'Doug's doing well. They're going to keep him in for a few more days, review his drugs and then send him back.'

'We're going to have to add him to our cardiac rehab list,' Kyla said, her eyes still on Ethan. 'We need to try and get him to take some exercise. Evanna runs a class at the community centre once a week. When he's recovered, I'll talk to him about it.'

'It's Leslie who is going to need the support.' Logan winced as Kirsty grabbed another hunk of hair. 'She rang me from the hospital with loads of questions.'

'Don't they answer questions in hospital?'

Logan gave a laugh. 'She doesn't trust them. She wanted to hear it from me.'

Kyla rolled her eyes. 'What's it like to enjoy such godlike status?'

'Exhausting. Leslie is coming back over

tomorrow to check on Andrea. She's staying with a schoolfriend but obviously she was pretty upset about the whole thing and worried about her dad. Those prawns are done, Ethan. There's a plate there and some of Evanna's lemon mayonnaise on the side. Help yourself.'

'Bit of a handful, our Andrea, by all accounts.' Kyla reached for a plate and held it while Ethan removed the prawns from the barbecue.

The tension in his body had lessened and Kyla watched as he shelled prawns and drank beer, chatting to Logan and occasionally tending the barbecue.

Had it been her imagination?

Maybe. Certainly he seemed fine now and he even handed Kirsty some bread to chew.

'I had Sonia Davies from the library in my antenatal clinic today,' Evanna said, speaking directly to Logan. 'She really wants a home birth.'

The smile faded from Logan's face. 'I won't do home births,' he said gruffly, 'you know that. Don't even bother asking me.'

Evanna bit her lip. 'It's her second baby and she's—'

'I won't do home births.'

'Logan, she isn't—'

'She can go to the community maternity unit on the mainland. It has all the advantages of home births, with none of the risks. This is an island, Evanna. I know you'll tell me that if something happens she can be transferred, but will it be fast enough? We do wonders here, but we have to be realistic. I can't provide neonatal intensive care and neither can I perform uterine surgery on a woman with an uncontrollable hae-morrhage.' His tone harsh, Logan turned away and helped himself to another beer. Evanna glanced helplessly at Kyla, who gave a brief shake of her head to indicate that she should drop the subject.

They both knew what was behind Logan's intransigence. Catherine.

Feeling awful for him, Kyla strolled over to her brother and put a hand on his arm. 'Mum rang last night.' She kept her tone neutral. Steady. 'She's thinking of coming back over for Dad's birthday and spending a few days with her grandchild. They're missing her terribly. They loved the last set of photos you sent, especially the one of her sitting in the laundry basket.'

He was silent for a moment and then he breathed out heavily and she saw his shoulders relax. 'It would be good if they came. Kirsty loves to see them.'

'Mum's worried she's missing all the best bits.' Kyla gave his arm a gentle squeeze and then let go and helped herself to a baby tomato. 'I just hope she's here when Kirsty takes her first steps or we'll never hear the last of it.'

Logan's eyes settled on hers and she smiled gently, watching as some of the strain left his face. 'I'm all right,' he said roughly in Gaelic, and she gave a brief nod and replied in the same language.

'I know you're all right.'

And then she turned and caught Ethan

looking at them, a curious expression on his handsome face.

He was a complex character, she thought as she strolled back over to Evanna. Deep. A real thinker. But that didn't mean anything was wrong.

She thought back to the way he'd looked when he'd first seen Kirsty.

It had just been her imagination working overtime, Kyla decided, her face brightening as one of her aunts arrived along with two of her cousins. She'd spent too long listening to Evanna's gloomy observations.

Ethan was a serious person, there was little doubt about that.

Some people were.

That didn't mean he had demons.

CHAPTER FIVE

THE next two weeks passed so quickly that it seemed to Kyla that they hardly had time to breathe between patients.

Doug McDonald came home from hospital, very subdued and worried about doing anything, and Kyla called in every day to check on his progress and reassure him. She knew that Ethan had called several times, too, and was pleased that he'd bothered.

Two weeks had been enough to prove to her that he was an excellent doctor. He'd settled into the routine and seemed to have no problem handling even the trickiest of cases. Remembering how some previous locums had panicked at being confronted by such complex cases with no local hospital support, Kyla was impressed.

But she still didn't feel she was any closer to knowing or understanding him.

He ran on the beach every morning as the sun rose, pounding hard across the sand and up onto the cliffs, pushing himself to the limit. Then he'd return to the cottage, shower and drive up to the village in time for morning surgery.

He was serious and committed but revealed absolutely nothing about himself to anyone.

Occasionally he joined her and Logan for supper and sometimes she saw him on his own in the garden, sitting on his own, staring out to sea.

Perhaps that was what came of living in a big anonymous city where you were one of millions, Kyla thought. You forgot how to relate to your fellow man.

She was clearing up after an immunisation clinic when Janet buzzed through and asked if she'd see an extra patient.

'It's Mary Hillier. She wants you to take a

look at Shelley. Logan's gone out on a call and Ethan is back to back with patients so I don't like to bother him.'

Kyla thought of the six calls she had to make and the paperwork waiting for her attention. 'Of course, Janet. Send her in.'

She couldn't remember the last time Mary had come to the clinic for anything other than routine checks so the fact that she was asking for an appointment meant that she was must be really worried about something.

She tipped a syringe and needles into the sharps box and washed her hands just as Mary tapped on the door and walked in.

'Sorry to bother you, Nurse MacNeil,' she said in a formal voice, gently pushing Shelley into the room. 'I just wondered if you'd take a look at something for me.'

'Of course. What's the problem?'

'It's not me, it's Shelley. She's got these bruises all over her.'

'Bruises?' Kyla smiled at the girl. 'How are

you, Shelley? I saw you play in that netball match at the beginning of term. You were fantastic.'

Shelley blushed. 'You were watching?'

'I came down to give a talk to some of the children on healthy eating and I couldn't resist poking my nose in. So, where are these bruises? Can you show me?'

Shelley hesitated and then lifted her top. 'They're everywhere, really. And I've got these on my legs.' She slid her trouser legs up and Kyla bent down to take a closer look.

'How long have you had them?'

'They've just come up in the last few days,' Shelley muttered. 'At first I thought I'd just banged myself, but now they're everywhere so I don't think it's that. I didn't fall or anything.'

'Have you been ill, Shelley?' Kyla reached for a thermometer and checked the girl's temperature.

'No. Nothing.'

Mary looked anxiously at Kyla. 'Does she have a temperature?'

Kyla shook her head and forced a smile that

she hoped was reassuring. 'No. Her temperature is fine. Why don't we ask the doctor to take a look at her? I'm just going to pop across to Dr Walker and see if he can fit her in.'

She left the room but Mary caught up with her in the corridor. 'Nurse MacNeil…'

Kyla turned and saw the worry in the other woman's face. She reached out and touched her on the arm, acknowledging the concern. 'I doubt it's what you're thinking, Mary,' she said softly, 'but we'll get it checked out immediately. Dr Walker is very, very good. If there's anything for us to be worrying about, he'll tell us soon enough. He trained at one of the top London hospitals, you know. You go back to Shelley or she'll pick up on your worry.'

Mary bit her lip but gave a nod and returned to the treatment room.

Kyla knocked on Ethan's door and walked in.

He was reading something on the computer screen and had a pen in his hand. 'Yes?'

'It's me. And you can put that frown away,

Dr Walker, because I don't scare easily.' She kept her tone light and saw a glimmer of a smile in his eyes.

'I'm sure you don't. Can I do something for you?' He was wearing a dark, well-cut suit and he looked formal and more than a little remote.

'I hope so.' Trying not to be intimidated by the suit, Kyla came straight to the point. 'I've a patient I'm worried about. Eleven-year-old girl with bruising all over her body. My first reaction is to panic and think meningitis, but she looks well, apart from a bit tired, perhaps. Her temperature is normal and she's not been ill.'

'If meningitis even floats through your head, I'll see her straight away.' Ethan put the pen down on the desk and stood up. 'What's your second reaction?'

Relieved and impressed that he was taking her so seriously, Kyla came straight out with it. 'Leukaemia. I don't want to be dramatic but it has to cross your mind, doesn't it?'

'There are many possible diagnoses,' Ethan

said calmly as he walked round the desk. 'Leukaemia is just one.'

'I know, but—' Kyla broke off and bit her lip. 'You should know that Shelley's mother, Mary, had a sister with leukaemia. She died about three years ago. Mary hasn't asked a direct question and obviously she doesn't want to frighten the child, but I can see from her eyes that she's frantic with worry.'

Ethan walked towards the door. 'Then the sooner I see her, the better. I'll have a better idea once I've examined her and obviously I'm going to need to do some blood tests. Bring her in.' His tone was crisp. Direct. 'I'll examine her here. And you'd better stay, if you have the time, given that you know the history.'

'I'll stay.' She wasn't going anywhere until she knew what was happening.

Ethan examined the child thoroughly, aware of the tension in Mary's body as she stood to the side of him, watching.

He questioned Shelley at length and then smiled at her. 'I'm going to need to take some blood from you, just to run a few routine tests. Is that all right?'

Shelley pulled a face. 'Will it hurt?'

'A bit,' Ethan said honestly, reaching behind him for the tray he'd prepared. 'But not much and not for long. Kyla?'

Kyla handed him a tourniquet and he tightened it round the girl's arm, stroking the skin as he searched for a good vein.

Kyla kept up a steady stream of chat. 'So did your netball team go over to the mainland and play the girls at St Jude's last week?'

A smile spread across Shelley's face. 'We thrashed them. Sixteen to one.'

'Brilliant.' Kyla turned to Ethan. 'The school is so small here that every single girl is in the netball team!'

'But we're still the best,' Shelley said quickly, and Ethan smiled, mentally blessing Kyla for her distraction skills.

'Sharp scratch coming up, Shelley,' he said smoothly, and slid the needle into the vein.

Shelley didn't stop talking. 'Mia Wilson was the best. She got it in the net about fourteen times.'

'Well, she's tall, of course, so that helps,' Kyla murmured, handing him a piece of cotton wool. 'And her mum is the sports teacher, which is another distinct advantage.'

Shelley laughed and Ethan withdrew the needle and pressed with the cotton wool.

'I'll do that while you sort out the sample,' Kyla murmured, her fingers sliding over his as she took over the pressure.

Her hands were so much smaller than his, her fingers slim and delicate and Ethan felt a sudden burst of heat erupt inside him.

Gritting his teeth and rejecting the feeling, he turned away and labelled the samples carefully. 'I'm going to send these off. As soon as I get a result, I'll be in touch.' Seeing the anxiety in Mary's eyes, he turned to Kyla. 'Can you take Shelley to your treatment room and find her a plaster, please? I don't seem to have one here.'

To her credit, Kyla immediately picked up on his intention. 'Useless doctors,' she said cheerfully, slipping her arm through Shelley's and leading her towards the door. 'They can do all sorts of fancy, complicated things but when it comes to something simple like a plaster, you can forget it. We girls will see you in Reception in a minute.'

Ethan waited until the door closed behind them and then turned to Mary. 'I understand that you're very worried about this.'

Mary was stiff, her fingers gripping her handbag. 'Do I have reason to be?'

'Obviously, until I have the results back, I can't be sure what it is, but I'm pretty confident that it isn't leukaemia.'

Mary's teeth clamped on her lips and he could see that she was battling with tears. 'If it is—'

'I don't think it is,' Ethan said firmly. 'There are other things that it can be, Mrs Hillier. I'm going to get these results back as fast as possible and then I'll call you. Is it useless to tell you not to worry?'

'Completely useless.' Mary gave a wan smile. 'But thank you for your thoughtfulness.'

'So you don't think it's leukaemia?' Kyla closed the door of his consulting room and stood with her back to it. 'Really?'

'Shelley looks well and there's no history of trauma. I've examined her thoroughly and her liver and spleen feel normal and there's no evidence of lymphadenopathy.'

'So what are the bruises?'

'Obviously until I see the results of the blood count I can't be sure, but I think she probably has ITP. Idiopathic thrombocytopenic purpura.'

Kyla frowned. 'I've heard of it but I don't know much about it and we've certainly never had a patient. What's the treatment?'

'Depending on the platelet count, it may just be a case of watchful waiting. In someone of

Shelley's age the condition will probably be acute and it will resolve over a few months.'

'And if it doesn't?'

He gave a faint smile. 'What's happened to your cheerful, optimistic nature, Kyla?'

'I just like to know the options.' She looked away, struggling with her body's powerful response to his smile. He was indecently attractive. 'Mary is a friend of my mother's. She had Shelley late in life and she's very precious. I need to have all the facts at my disposal.'

'In a small number of children it can be chronic, and she might have to avoid contact sports...' he shrugged '...but so much depends on the blood tests. If her platelets are at a reasonable level then it becomes less of a problem. It's really too soon to try and predict the future for her.'

'So you're saying that she could just recover spontaneously?'

'That's right.' He studied her closely. 'You look as worried and upset as her mother. It doesn't do to get too involved with your patients, Nurse MacNeil.'

His comment stung and her shoulders stiffened defensively. 'Well, that's the theory certainly.' She lifted her chin. 'Try living on an island where you know everyone, Dr Walker. And, then try staying detached. It's a pretty tall order, I can tell you. And frankly, I don't think I'd like to be the sort of person who didn't care what happened to her patients.'

He frowned. 'Kyla—'

'And now, if you'll excuse me, I have things to do.' She tugged open the door and left the room, taking several deep breaths in an attempt to control her temper. How dared he suggest that she was too involved with her patients?

She cared about them.

What was wrong with that?

Thoroughly unsettled, she went back to her own consulting room and finished the clearing-up she'd started before Janet had asked her to see Shelley.

Infuriating man, she thought as she pushed a box of dressings back into the cupboard and slammed the door shut. He may be amazing to look at but he was cold-hearted and unemotional. Which made him completely wrong for her.

Evanna was right.

It would be safer to steer clear of him.

Ethan vaulted over the fence that separated the two cottages and walked up the garden.

The doors to the kitchen were open and he could see Kyla standing in front of the stove, singing along to the radio. Her blonde curls were pinned haphazardly to the top of her head and her feet were bare. She wore a pair of faded jeans that rode low on her hips, exposing a tempting expanse of smooth, tanned abdomen. She was lean, fit and incredibly sexy, and something dangerous stirred inside him.

He gritted his teeth and reminded himself that he couldn't afford the luxury of becoming involved with this woman.

Life was about to become complicated enough without the extra dimension that a relationship would inevitably bring.

He was just working out the best way to begin what needed to be said when she glanced up and saw him. The singing stopped.

'I have a perfectly good front door with a working doorbell.'

'I heard you singing so I thought I'd come round the back.' He ignored her frosty tone and strolled into the kitchen. 'You can stop glaring at me because I've come to apologise.'

'You're saying that you were wrong?'

'No.' She had beautiful eyes, he decided. In fact, the whole package was beautiful. 'I still think it doesn't do to get too involved with patients, but I can see that it might be hard to do that on an island like this. And you're very caring, there's no doubt about that.' And it was impossible not to respond to her.

Suddenly he wanted to touch her. *Really touch*

her. He wanted to taste and feel and immerse himself in the woman she was.

'Caring is what makes this community so special.'

'I'm sure that's true. But isn't it also true that caring too much sometimes makes it difficult to do your job?'

A shadow darkened her blue eyes and her slim shoulders sagged slightly. 'Perhaps. But it's hard to change your personality, Ethan. You just have to work with what you've got. This is me. This is who I am.' Her simple statement encompassed the differences between them and guilt gnawed at his insides.

She was open and honest. Transparent.

Whereas he…

Her quiet declaration reminded him that she knew nothing about the person he really was.

He clenched his hands into fists by his sides to stop himself from reaching out and hauling her against him. To make any sort of move would be inexcusable when he was hiding so much from her.

Cold and hard were adjectives that many women had applied to him but so far no one had thrown 'immoral' at him, and he didn't intend them to start now.

'I just think that you can do your job better if you can stay slightly detached. It makes it easier to think clearly.'

She gave a sigh and turned back to the pan on the hob. 'You sound like Logan. He always manages to get the balance right. I'm terrible. I take everything much more personally, but I can't help it.'

'And that's what makes you a nice person.' He realised that it was true. Even during the short time he'd been on the island he could see that she gave a great deal of herself to her job and to the community. 'What are you cooking?'

'Soup from a can. I can hardly bear the anticipation.' She stared at the gloopy liquid with a distinct lack of enthusiasm. 'I'd offer you some but frankly I wouldn't want to poison you. You're better off with whatever you have in your own fridge.'

'There's nothing in my fridge apart from milk and beer and neither of those is going to make a decent meal. Is there a good pub on the island?'

'The Stag's Head. Down on the quay. Given that they know what you did for Doug, I doubt you'd even have to pay for your supper. You'll probably get a hero's welcome.'

'I don't mind paying but I need to eat something soon. I missed lunch.' He leaned forward and turned off the hob. 'Let's go.'

She stared at him and then at the saucepan on the hob. 'I'm eating soup.'

'Not any more. You're eating in the pub with me.'

Her eyes narrowed. 'What if I don't want to eat in the pub?'

'You'd rather eat congealed soup of indeterminate origin?' He watched her shudder and gave a smile. 'Come on. We both know that a stranger walking into that place is going to be given the third degree. If you're so committed to helping people in the community, the least you can do is give me some moral support.'

She looked at the soup and then back at him. 'It isn't that hard a choice.'

'Good.' He glanced down at her feet. 'Just put some shoes on or the locals will talk.'

And he hoped she'd change out of the jeans in order to allow his blood pressure to settle.

Kyla walked into the pub ahead of Ethan and felt every pair of eyes in the room fasten themselves on her.

Let them talk, she thought cheerfully, elbowing her way to the bar through the crowd of locals. It had been a long time since anyone had had reason to gossip about her. It would do them all good. 'Coming through,' she sang out as she wiggled and pushed her way to the front. 'This is a medical emergency. Starving hungry and gasping for a drink.'

The man behind the bar grinned and opened a fridge. 'So this is for medicinal purposes?'

'Of course, Ben. What else?' She settled herself on a stool at the bar and rested her arms on the bar.

Ben handed her a glass of white wine. 'We were all shocked to hear about Doug.'

'Logan spoke to the hospital today and he's doing all right. He'll be home before you know it.'

'All the same, I feel responsible.' Ben scratched his head awkwardly and Kyla looked at him quizzically.

'How can you possibly be responsible?'

'He was lugging my crates around,' Ben said roughly, and Kyla gave a soft smile.

'And from what I heard, you were the one to take him straight to the surgery, so you did him a good turn. Stop fretting.' Kyla glanced behind her and noticed that Ethan was hovering on the edge of the crowd. On impulse, she ordered for him and pushed her way back through to a vacant table, clutching the glasses. 'I ordered you a pint of the local brew. Hope that's OK. We'll sit here.'

'I feel like a zoo animal on display. Do they ever stop staring?'

'Only when someone more interesting walks in. Here. Try this.' Kyla handed him the drink. 'It will put hairs on your chest.'

His eyes met hers and she felt her heart skip a beat. *Now, why had she said a stupid thing like that when she was trying so hard not to think about his body?*

'Unless you want the whole island gossiping, I suggest you stop looking at me like that,' he suggested in a soft tone, and lifted the glass and drank.

'I am not looking at you. You're looking at me. And if I walk into the pub with a man, people are going to gossip. It's a fact of life.'

He put his drink back down on the table. 'Sorry. I'm not used to being the centre of attention.'

Wasn't he? Kyla was willing to lay bets that wherever he went women stared at him, but perhaps he just wasn't aware of that fact. 'Does it bother you?'

'No. Does it bother you?'

She smiled. 'I've lived here for most of my life. I'm used to it. But I know that it drove Catherine potty sometimes.'

He looked at her. 'What was she like?'

'Oh…' She wondered why he was interested. 'Lively, a bit on the wild side, flirtatious, quite amusing. She had a sharp tongue and she wasn't terribly patient.'

'How did she meet Logan?'

'She was travelling and arrived on the island one day. They met. Hit it off. Catherine became pregnant. They got married—and, yes, that was all in the wrong order so don't start my mother on that topic—and then…' Kyla broke off and sighed. 'And then it all went wrong.'

'And that's why Logan doesn't encourage women to have home births?'

'Can you blame him? Not that Catherine was

booked to have a home birth, anyway, but, given what happened, Logan wants every woman safely on the mainland the moment she starts to dilate.'

'And Evanna disagrees?'

'Evanna is a midwife. She wants to give every woman the birth experience they want. But she accepts the limitations of living somewhere like this. You can tell yourself that the helicopter can come and fly you out in an emergency, but what if the weather is bad, or there's been another accident somewhere and they can't get out to you?'

'I can understand Logan's reluctance.'

'He won't even consider it, and the women here respect that. To be honest, most of them want the reassurance of giving birth in a consultant-led unit so we don't get that many requests. I am completely starving. I need to order before I faint.' She turned and squinted over her shoulder towards the blackboard on the wall. 'The food here is amazing. See anything you fancy?'

'Why don't you choose for both of us? But I ought to warn you that I hate haggis.'

'That's because you're a soft Englishman.' She caught the eye of Jim, the ferryman, who was downing a pint with one of the local fishermen. He winked at her and she smiled broadly. 'Have the beef Wellington. It's amazing.'

'I feel as though I'm in a goldfish bowl,' Ethan said mildly. 'How does anyone ever have a relationship in a place like this? It's impossible to keep anything private.'

'The relationship bit is all right,' Kyla said easily, reaching for her wine. 'It's the private bit that presents more of a challenge. You just have to ignore it. And, anyway, we're not having a relationship. We're just colleagues, out for a civilised meal.'

His eyes held hers. 'That's right. So we are.'

It was impossible to look away. *Impossible not to feel the powerful spark of chemistry that drew them together.* She saw his mouth tighten and sensed his growing tension. 'We should order.'

'Yes.' He dragged his eyes away from hers and glanced over to the bar. 'I presume I have to fight my way through the crowd for that pleasure?'

'Actually, you don't.' Ben, the landlord, was standing next to them, a grin on his face as he looked at them. 'After what you did for Doug this morning, you're right at the front of our queue.'

'We'll both have the beef,' Kyla said quickly, 'and the treacle tart. Thanks, Ben.'

He scribbled on the pad in his hand. 'How's young Shelley?'

'Fine.'

'Mary's worrying herself sick.'

'I know that.' Kyla's voice was quiet. 'We're dealing with it as quickly as we can, Ben. As soon as we know anything, we'll be in touch with Mary.'

He nodded. 'Call me when you hear anything.' He walked off and Ethan stared after him in amazement.

'How did he know about Shelley? And how does he know so much about Doug? And how do you ever honour patient confidentiality in a place like this?'

'Doug works for him and Ben is Mary's cousin, but you're right that most people find out who's ill with what about five seconds after you've found out yourself. Anyway, Ben is on the crew of Glenmore lifeboat so he's an important part of this community.'

'The island has a lifeboat?'

'Yes. It has a berth by the quay. Haven't you seen it?'

'I haven't been down here since the day I arrived. Do they have a lot of callouts?'

'Unfortunately, yes. Especially in the summer. Usually walkers on the cliffs who drop down to pretty bays and then get stuck when the tide comes in. And if it's a medical emergency, they call on Logan. So, you see, we all work together and, yes, people are interested in one another, but we don't betray a confidence. There's a way of responding without giving anything away. But I can assure you that the moment you've spoken to Mary about the results, she'll be on the phone to at least five other people and they'll be on the phone to another five. But that's their business.'

Ethan shook his head. 'It's so different to London.'

'Of course. That's why we live here.' She tilted her head to one side, challenging him. 'You're missing all the positives. Like the fact that almost everyone on this island is part of an informal support network and that counts for a lot. When Fraser was in hospital with pneumonia when he was younger, everyone rallied round to help Aisla, even though she'd only just arrived on the island and knew no one.'

He sat back in his chair, his expression watchful. 'Go on.'

She shrugged. 'When Mrs Linton tripped down her stairs someone phoned us within the hour because they'd noticed that her bin hadn't been taken in. In London she probably would have been on the floor for a week before it occurred to anyone that something might be wrong.'

'Probably even longer than that,' Ethan said dryly, finishing his drink and sitting back as their food arrived. 'All right, you've convinced me. I can see that it has its advantages.'

'But it isn't somewhere that you could ever settle for good.' The words left her mouth before she could stop them and she froze, appalled at herself for being so indiscreet.

Why had she asked that question? What was the matter with her? It wasn't even as if she wanted him to be there for ever. She just wanted—she wanted—

A fling, she acknowledged finally, looking away from his searching gaze so that she didn't reveal any more. She wanted a wild, abandoned fling with an incredible-looking, intelligent man, and Ethan Walker fitted that description.

'What about you?' His voice was even as he handed her a knife and fork and reached for his own. 'You're obviously an extremely skilled nurse. Have you ever considered leaving here?'

'What's that supposed to mean? That the people on the island deserve less than mainlanders?'

'That wasn't what I meant.' His tone was wry. 'You're very touchy. Stop jumping down my throat. I just wondered whether you might be bored.'

'I trained on the mainland and that was enough for me. Here I have a great deal more autonomy than I would have on the mainland. I happen to think that anonymity is vastly over-rated.' She poked the food on her plate for a moment and then looked up. 'I like people, Ethan. I like knowing what they're up to. I don't even mind the fact that they know everything that I'm doing before I even do it. I like the feeling of belonging. I like the knowledge that there is a whole community out there, pulling together, trying to improve each other's lives. In cities all you read about is stabbings and muggings, whereas here—' She broke off and gave an embarrassed shrug.

'I sense that we're back to caring again.'

'They probably care in the city, too, it's just that life is so fast and busy that no one has the opportunity to show it, and before you know it you don't even recognise your neighbours.'

'Is that really an excuse?' Ethan gave a short laugh. 'You're not exactly kicking your heels here and you manage to know everyone.'

'But we have a pretty static population except for the tourist season. Live in a city and people come and go. Here, everyone we see here is known to us. It's different. And I love the challenge of having to work with limited back-up. It makes you more resourceful.'

They'd both finished eating and Kyla suddenly realised that she'd been too absorbed in their conversation to even notice the food. 'Did you enjoy it?'

His surprised glance at his empty plate told her that he'd been similarly distracted.

'Very much. The treacle tart was delicious.'

'Shall I order some coffee?'

Ethan looked at her. 'Let's have coffee at

home. That way we can drink it without everyone watching.'

She smiled. 'Good plan.'

What had possessed him to suggest coffee when what he really needed was to keep as far away from her as possible?

Frustrated with himself, Ethan walked briskly back towards the cottages and resolved to make the coffee quick and businesslike. If he kept the conversation fairly formal, that would help.

And he wouldn't look at her.

'Ethan? Are you OK?' Kyla's voice had a soft, breathy quality and he suddenly realised that not looking at her wasn't going to make any difference at all. He could have had his eyes shut in a dark room and she still would have had the same effect on him.

'I'm fine.' He could feel her looking at him and lengthened his stride. 'How is Doug doing anyway? Did Logan get any feedback from the hospital?'

'Oh. Better, I think. Seems a bit more relaxed. It's Leslie who's the problem. She's hanging over him every minute of the day, just waiting for him to collapse. I'm going round there tomorrow to see if I can help her get her head around the whole thing.'

This was fine, Ethan told himself as they reached the cottages. *This was good.* Talking about work kept everything on a safe level. He could handle this. Quick coffee. Small talk. And he wasn't going to touch her.

His resolve lasted as long as it took to follow her into her kitchen.

She was still wearing the jeans but she'd added a pair of sexy heels and a pretty cardigan in a shade of blue that matched her eyes.

'I'll put the kettle on,' she said cheerfully, reaching for mugs and coffee, 'and we can take it down to the beach if you like. It's lovely to sit on the sand in the dark and watch the stars.'

He felt a sudden rush of heat through his body.

'Here is fine,' he said hoarsely, running a hand over the back of his neck. He didn't need the darkness or stars. 'The kitchen is fine.' *There was nothing romantic about fluorescent light.*

'All right. If that's what you prefer.' She shot him a curious look and spooned fresh coffee into a cafetière. 'Do you realise that you've been here for two weeks and I still know hardly anything about you? We've been so busy we've hardly exchanged more than two words.'

And that was the way he'd wanted it. 'There's not much to know about me.'

'You mean there's not much you want to tell.' She poured water into the pot. 'Where did you work last?'

Hell? 'Abroad.'

She gave a soft laugh and turned to face him. 'You don't give anything away, do you, Ethan? Did anyone ever tell you that one-word answers don't make a conversation?'

'I'm not that great at conversation. You should have worked that out by now.' She had the bluest eyes he'd ever seen and her legs looked impossibly long. 'I ought to go…'

She hesitated and then walked towards him, narrowing the distance that he'd carefully placed between them. 'You haven't drunk your coffee.'

He wasn't even sure who touched who first.

He just knew that one moment he was standing there full of good intentions and then next she had her arms wrapped round his neck and his mouth was hard on hers.

His good intentions dissolved, as did his conscience and all the other better parts of his nature that had been holding him back.

His hands traced the soft curves that his eyes had already admired. His mouth devouring hers, he slid his hands over her hips, then over her bottom, anchoring her against him. The taste and the scent of her threatened to overwhelm him and he dragged his mouth away from hers and pressed his lips against her neck.

'Ethan…' She murmured his name and

pressed closer and that movement alone was enough to snap the last of his self-control.

His mouth found hers again and his hands moved to the hem of her top, sliding underneath, finding the smooth, tanned skin that he'd admired earlier.

Her breasts pressed into his hands and he almost lost control as he felt her nipples peak under the brush of his fingers and heard her soft gasp of pleasure.

He lifted his head and their mouths met again in a fierce kiss, each demanding of the other, each hungry and possessive and increasingly desperate. His entire body was consumed by a ferocious heat and he felt her hands shaking as they struggled with the buttons on his shirt.

It was the touch of her fingers against his bare chest that brought him to his senses.

Another minute more and neither of them would have stopped.

'Kyla…' With difficulty he broke his mouth from hers and forced his hands to release her smooth, golden flesh '…we have to stop. This isn't a good idea.'

She gave a whimper of protest and leaned in towards him again, but he stepped backwards, breathing heavily.

'Kyla, no.'

She blinked, her eyes dazed and disorientated. 'Why—? What?' Her mouth was soft and bruised from his kiss and he gritted his teeth and reminded himself that she knew nothing about him.

She didn't know who he was or why he was there. But when she did… 'Trust me. This is a mistake.'

She took a step back and when she spoke, her voice was soft. 'Did it feel like a mistake, Ethan?'

Physically, no. But he had more sense than to take that route given the present set of circumstance. 'We need to forget this happened.'

'Why?' Her blue eyes studied his face, searching for answers to the questions bubbling up inside her. 'This wasn't just me, it was you, too.'

'I know that.'

'Then—'

'I can't explain, but it isn't you, it's me,' he growled, reaching for the door like a drowning man would have grasped anything that happened to float. 'And now I need to go home.'

'But—'

'Goodnight, Kyla. Thanks for dinner.'

He didn't wait to hear her reply, just strode out of her cottage and kept his eyes on his own front door.

Once there he switched on the kitchen light and pulled out the letter.

If nothing else, at least it would remind him of the reason he was there.

CHAPTER SIX

HE STRODE into her consulting room next morning with a piece of paper in his hand.

'I've had the blood results on Shelley.'

Kyla stared at him. That was it?

They'd shared a kiss that had probably shaken the foundations of the island and *that was all he had to say?*

Her heart thundering at a dangerous pace, she waited for him to make some reference to the previous evening, but he was remote and businesslike. Cold. *Unapproach-able.* It was as if the kiss had never happened.

Clearly he hadn't suffered the same restless night that she had.

Kyla sighed inwardly, still unable to believe

that he'd stopped so abruptly. The question was why? Evanna was obviously right. He had issues. It was just frustrating that he was unwilling to share them. Deciding that this wasn't the time or the place to try and fight him, she looked at him expectantly. 'And what do her results say?'

'It's definitely ITP. But her platelet levels are reasonable so hopefully it will resolve by itself in a few months. I've had a chat with the haematologist and his advice is to do nothing for the time being. We'll check her blood again regularly and see how she goes.'

'That's good news.' Kyla's relief was genuine. 'Mary will be delighted to hear all that.'

'I've called them and asked them to come to surgery this afternoon. Five o'clock. I thought you might like to be there.'

'I would. Thanks.' Was he ever going to mention the kiss they'd shared or was it just going to be consigned to the archives without further reference? Was that the usual end to an evening out for him? Did he kiss women like that all the time?

As if reading her thoughts, his eyes moved to hers and her heart started to beat faster. His mouth tightened and he cleared his throat. 'I need to get on.'

'Yes. Of course you do.' Her voice was a croak and he sucked in a breath and turned away from her, yanking open the door and leaving the room with a purposeful stride.

He was always walking away from her.

Kyla stared after him in mounting frustration. She wanted to run after him and ask the questions that were hovering on her lips.

What are you playing at?

Aren't you going to say anything about the kiss?

Are you going to ignore what's happening between the two of us?

Or maybe she'd imagined the whole thing and he just didn't find her attractive. 'Men,' she muttered to herself, cleaning the dressing trolley ready for her next patient. 'How can they accuse us women of being confusing?'

She tried to keep her mind focussed on the job all day and then at five o'clock she joined Ethan in his consulting room.

'Mary and Shelley are just coming.' She looked at him, trying not to be intimidated by his cool, formal appearance. 'You're wearing a suit again.'

He gave a faint smile. 'I'm at work.'

'And does the suit help you keep the distance you need from people?' She asked the question without thinking and then immediately wished she'd kept her mouth shut when he looked at her steadily.

'This isn't the right time, Kyla.' His voice was soft and she felt the colour rush into her cheeks because she knew it wasn't the right time and she was furious with herself for even showing that she cared.

She wished she had the ability to be as indifferent as he obviously was.

Hurt and confused, she turned as she heard a tap on the door.

Mary Hillier walked in with Shelley, and Ethan immediately waved a hand at the two chairs he'd placed next to the desk. 'Sit down. I can see you're worried so let's get straight to the point.' He outlined the results of the blood tests, explaining in simple, precise language.

Mary was looking relieved. 'So tell me more about this ITP thing. What exactly does it mean?'

'It means that there aren't enough platelets in the blood. If you cast your mind back to biology, you'll remember that platelets are responsible for helping the blood to clot.'

'So if she doesn't have enough platelets, she could bleed?'

'That's right. That's why she has more bruising than usual.'

'And what's caused it?'

'It's an autoimmune disease. In other words, your body attacks itself—in this case it attacks the platelets. As to what causes it—most of the experts think that in children it's caused by a viral infection.'

'But there's no treatment? You're not going to do anything?'

'Treatment isn't always necessary, particularly in children. They tend to recover completely in a couple of months without any intervention.'

'But what if she has problems?'

Ethan reached for a pen and scribbled something on a pad. 'This is my number.' He handed the paper to Mary. 'If you can't get me in surgery, feel free to call me on that number if you have any worries. We will be checking Shelley's blood regularly to see if the platelet count is recovering.'

Kyla nodded her approval. He may be dressed in a suit and look unapproachable, but he was making himself accessible to worried patients and they didn't seem to find him intimidating.

Mary folded the paper and put it carefully in her handbag. 'And does she need to stop doing sport or anything? She loves her netball and they're playing loads of matches at school at the moment.'

'The way her platelet count is at the moment, it's fine for her to play.' Ethan scribbled something else on the pad. 'We'll monitor it and if it drops to a certain level then we may need to advise you to avoid contact sports, but at the moment it's fine just to carry on as normal.'

A relieved Mary left the room and Kyla managed a smile.

'You're very good at explaining.'

'Despite the suit?' There was humour in his eyes but she was too confused by her own feelings to respond.

'Thanks for spending so much time with them,' she said quickly, making for the door. She needed to escape. The effect he had on her was profoundly unsettling, but it was clear that he didn't feel the same way and the sooner she came to terms with that, the better for both of them. 'I need to get on.'

'Kyla, wait.'

She didn't turn but her grip tightened on the

doorhandle. 'Not now, Ethan,' she said quietly, keeping her eyes forward. *Looking ahead.* 'As you said yourself, this isn't the right time.'

Ethan stared after her, feeling the frustration rise inside him.

Why now?

Why her and why now?

He lifted a hand to the knot of his tie and loosened it with a vicious jerk as he cursed softly.

He'd hurt her feelings. She thought he'd rejected her, and in a way he had, but only because he wasn't in a position to do anything else.

He turned and stared out of the window, watching the first threatening clouds appear in the sky.

He could tell her the truth, of course. He could tell her who he was and why he was there.

But he wasn't able to do that yet.

He wasn't ready.

There were still so many things that he didn't understand and he needed time to work out the answers to all the questions he had. Then, maybe then, he could do something about Kyla MacNeil. *Soon.*

She felt such a fool.

Kyla slipped into the driver's seat of her car, stealing a glance at the low black sports car parked next to her. It was sleek, sophisticated and exclusive. Like its owner, she thought sadly as she started her own car and pulled out of the medical centre car park.

Ethan Walker would never fit into a place like this and he'd never be interested in a woman like her.

She frowned slightly as she analysed her own thoughts. *Pathetic,* she decided crossly, changing gear with rather more force than was necessary. She was being completely pathetic and selling herself short. It wasn't that she wasn't good enough for him, because she was. It was just that some relationships just weren't meant to happen, and this was obviously one of those. Yes, there was chemistry. *Amazing chemistry.* But their lives were different. They appreciated different things. They were just—different.

He drove a flashy sports car, he wore a suit to work—a suit that she guessed had probably cost more than two months of her salary.

And while there was no doubt that he was an excellent doctor and good with the patients, it was also true that he held himself apart. He was—she searched for the word—aloof? Sometimes when he joined them at Logan's for supper, she caught him watching them from the edges, almost as if he were studying them. But was that really so surprising?

She thought of the little he'd told her about his childhood. About his parents who had divorced. About how they hadn't been interested in him.

What must he make of her big, noisy, involved family? Was it surprising that he found them worth studying? He probably found them completely perplexing.

Kyla gave a sigh and decided to call in on Doug and Leslie. They needed the support and it would stop her dwelling on her own problems.

She was going to stop wanting Ethan, she decided as she pressed her foot to the accelerator and sped down the country road that led inland to the McDonalds' house.

She was going to stop watching from the window when he ran on the beach in the early mornings, she was going to stop finding excuses to go into his surgery to talk to him and she was going to stop dreaming about *that kiss*.

Everyone made mistakes, of course they did. But never let it be said that she didn't learn from hers.

Move on, Kyla.

She pulled up outside the McDonald house and walked to the front door without bothering to lock her car.

'Anyone home?' The front door was open and she pushed it open and stuck her head through. 'Hello?'

Leslie walked out of the kitchen. 'Come on in, Nurse MacNeil,' she said briskly, wiping her hands on her apron. 'Your patient is just sitting in the garden but he's been for a walk this afternoon, just like they said. Just a short one. Up and down the garden. The kettle's hot if I can tempt you to a cup of tea.'

'Fantastic,' Kyla said, following her into the kitchen. 'Lunch feels like nothing more than a distant memory.'

Leslie gave a cluck of disapproval. 'You all work too hard in that surgery, but we're grateful for it. I certainly don't know where we'd all be without you.' She hesitated. 'Doug and I owe you so much—and that new doctor, too. The hospital was very impressed with the treatment Doug had with you. They said that you probably saved his life.'

'We did our job, Leslie,' Kyla said gently, 'and you don't owe us anything. It's just good that Ben brought Doug to us so quickly.'

Leslie nodded. 'Ben's a good man, no doubt

about that. And now he's short-staffed at the pub, of course.'

'Ben will cope.' Kyla looked out of the window and saw Doug staring across the garden. 'How's he doing?'

'Well, he hasn't had any more pain but he's tired, of course. The hospital warned him that the drugs might make him tired. Said that Dr Walker could alter the dose if necessary.'

'Yes.' Kyla turned to her. 'I meant mentally. Doug's used to being very active. How is he coping with having to take it easy?'

'Well, he doesn't have much choice but I think he finds it frustrating.' Leslie stared at her husband for a moment and then gave a bright smile. 'Now, then. What was I doing? Tea. I'd offer you cake but when I came back from the hospital with Doug I went through the cupboards and threw out everything unhealthy. We've only fruit left to snack on.'

'I don't need cake, Leslie, thank you, and it's good to know that you're thinking about his diet.'

Leslie dropped teabags into a pot. 'Hard to think about anything else,' she muttered, and Kyla stepped closer and put a hand on her shoulder.

'Have you talked to anyone?'

'Me?' Leslie's hand shook and she sloshed boiling water over the side of the teapot. 'Why would I need to talk to anyone? I'm not the one who is sick.'

'This happened to you as well as him,' Kyla said quietly, taking the kettle from her and putting it safely back on the side. She reached for a cloth and mopped at the water. 'It's very stressful, seeing someone that you love suddenly taken ill. And you've had to stay strong for everyone. It must be incredibly hard.'

'I'm fine,' Leslie said briskly, her smile just a little too bright. 'You go on outside and check on Doug. I'll join you in a minute.'

'Actually, I wanted to talk to you first.'

'I'm not the ill one.' Leslie folded a teatowel with almost obsessive attention to detail and then her face crumpled and she curled her fingers around the soft cloth and gripped it hard. 'I keep waiting for him to die,' she confessed in a whisper. 'Every time he gets out of that chair I want to stop him from moving just in case it causes a strain on his heart. I want to yell at him, "Don't move," and here they are telling him to start gentle exercise. They want him to do this cardiac rehab…something.'

'Rehabilitation.'

'That's right. Rehabilitation.' She sniffed. 'But I don't want him to lift a teacup, let alone exercise!'

'Oh, Leslie.' Her voice loaded with sympathy, Kyla stepped forward and gave the other woman a hug. 'The rehabilitation programme is really important after a heart attack. I know it seems scary to you but it's really important to gradually increase the amount of activity. They've looked at his age and his lifestyle and worked out what's right for him. I spoke to the cardiac sister this morning and we discussed the programme that the unit want him to follow.'

'He's got a video and some leaflets. And he's going to have to lose some of that weight.'

Kyla nodded. 'Yes, he is. But it's not just about diet and exercise, Leslie. It's about giving emotional support to both of you. About helping you both rebuild your lives.'

'Is that possible?'

'Yes.' Kyla's voice was soft. 'We're here for you, Leslie. You know we are. Logan, Dr Walker, Evanna and I. We're here. You're not on your own.'

'But you can't guarantee it will be OK, can you? You can't guarantee he won't have another one.'

'No,' Kyla said honestly, 'there are never any guarantees for anyone in this life. But we're going to do our best. Many people go on to lead full and long lives after a heart attack.'

'I can't even bear to sleep at night in case he needs me.'

'That's natural, Leslie. It's still very early days. You may not believe me now but that feeling will ease. You *will* grow more confident and both of you will eventually be back on your feet again. It won't go away but you'll be surprised how you manage to live with it. I've seen it happen before. I know at the moment this thing is dominating your lives, but as the weeks and months pass it will start to take more of a back seat.'

'Will it? I just keep picturing him lying on that couch with the oxygen mask on his face. I keep hearing all those machines beeping. I keep thinking of our little Andrea being left without a father—' Leslie broke off and covered her mouth with her hand, fighting back the tears.

'She still has her father,' Kyla said softly, 'and what you have to remember is that everyone is looking out for you. Both the doctors here and the hospital will be monitoring Doug and that's a good thing.'

'I hated those machines beeping in the hospital.' Leslie gave a humourless laugh. 'Now I'm missing them. At least when they were beeping I knew he was alive.'

'It's natural to feel a bit insecure when you're first discharged from hospital, but you're not on your own, Leslie. That's why we're here.'

'Leslie? Is that Kyla?' Doug's voice came from the garden and Leslie cleared her throat and turned on the tap to splash her face with cold water.

'Don't you go telling him I'm worried,' she said gruffly, drying her face with a towel and straightening her dress. 'I don't want him having any extra anxiety.'

'Do you think he doesn't know? Of course he knows you're worried!' Kyla shook her head and smiled. 'I'll go and chat to him while you take a moment for yourself. Maybe you can bring that tea out when you're ready.'

'I'll do that. And, Kyla…' Leslie's voice stopped her before she went through the back door.

'Yes?'

'Thank you, lass. You're a good girl.'

Kyla buried herself in work in an attempt not to think about Ethan.

She visited the McDonalds' most days on her way home and popped in on Aisla to check on her. She filled her clinics to the brim and saw everyone who wanted to be seen, usually on the same day. At night she fell into bed, exhausted. *And dreamed of Ethan.*

All his earlier reluctance to socialise with Logan and Kirsty seemed to have disappeared and he frequently joined Logan for supper, often in the garden and even turned up at Kirsty's first birthday party with an oversized stuffed teddy, which the little girl loved.

In order to avoid him, Kyla took to visiting Kirsty during the day and spending the occasional evening with her aunt who ran the café on the quay.

'You've been visiting us more than usual,' her aunt observed gently as she placed a bowl full of steaming home-made soup in front of Kyla. 'Is something wrong?'

'Nothing at all.' Kyla sniffed the bowl 'Smells

fantastic. Can you blame me for visiting? Given the choice of eating here or cooking for myself, there's no contest.'

'Kyla?' Her aunt sat down opposite her, ignoring the customers who had just streamed into the café from the ferry. 'I've known you all your life. There's something the matter, I can tell.'

'It's nothing.'

'And does this "nothing" happen to wear a suit and drive a flashy sports car?'

Kyla lifted her eyes from her soup. 'I don't know what you're talking about.'

'Don't you? This is an island, Kyla. It's hard for things to go on without anyone noticing.' Her aunt's voice was gentle as she stood up. 'You're entitled to your privacy, if that's what you want. But I'm reminding you that even though your mum's not around, you've still family here, Kyla Mary MacNeil. Family who love you. Don't you forget that.'

Kyla swallowed hard. 'He isn't interested, Aunty Meg.'

'Strikes me that he's a man with a great deal on his mind.'

Kyla gave a lopsided smile. 'You sound like Evanna. She thinks he has "issues".'

'Maybe he has. Maybe he just needs a bit of space to work a few things out and this is a good place for that.'

Kyla shook her head. 'I'm not pushing myself on him.'

'So is that why you're eating me out of house and home?' Meg pushed some more bread towards her. 'Because he's spending time with your brother and you're avoiding him?'

Kyla felt guilty. 'I love eating here and seeing you.'

Meg gave a snort. 'And do I need to be told that? Of course not. I'm not offended, lass, just worried about you.'

'You don't need to worry about me. I'm fine, really.' Kyla stood up to give her aunt a hug. 'Thanks.'

'Eat your supper.' Her aunt squeezed her gently and then released her. 'Before it gets cold.'

She loved her family. Kyla finished her soup, wondering if everyone else had noticed that she was suddenly spending all her time at the café instead of just strolling into Logan's garden in her usual fashion.

She thought about it all that night and the next day and when Evanna invited her to join them for a picnic on the beach that evening, she agreed.

She didn't want Logan making sarcastic comments, she thought as she slipped her feet into sandals, grabbed a cool-box and strolled down onto the sand.

Evanna was spreading a picnic out over a tartan rug while trying to control a thoroughly over-excited toddler. 'Don't eat sand,' she scolded gently, but there was a smile on her face as she scooped the little girl onto her lap and cuddled her. 'Go to your Aunty Kyla for a moment while I sort out the food.'

'I bought some things. It's just quiche and

salad.' Kyla put the cool-bag down by Evanna and stooped to kiss her niece.

Logan strolled over to her, his body glistening with seawater. 'It's fresh.'

'In other words, it's freezing.' Evanna laughed, handing him a towel. 'Quick. Dry yourself off. We don't want you developing hypothermia. It's a bad advert for the practice.'

Logan cast a questioning glance in Kyla's direction. 'Well, if it isn't my long-lost sister. Where have you been all week?' He dried himself and pulled a shirt over his head. 'I've hardly seen you.'

'I called in to see Aunty Meg a few times,' Kyla said casually, eating a tomato and then pulling a face. 'Ugh. Sand. Remind me whose idea was it to have a family picnic on the beach when it's windy? It always sounds such a great idea, but then you start to eat and you realise that everything is crunchy because it's full of sand. I think I prefer the garden.' She looked up to say something to Logan and saw Ethan strolling towards them. The words stuck in her throat.

'Kyla.' Evanna's voice was gentle. 'You're dropping food on the rug.'

Flustered, Kyla glanced down and realised that her hands were shaking so much she'd dropped the tomatoes. 'Sorry.' *She'd had no idea he was joining them.* Her heart skipped and danced and she gave herself a severe telling-off.

She'd avoided him for most of the week. She'd made a concerted effort not to look out of the window in the mornings and watch him run, and she'd even managed to forget about the kiss for at least five minutes at a stretch.

She'd thought she was doing well.

Only now, feeling her heart hammering hard against her chest, she knew that she wasn't doing well at all.

He affected her just as much as he ever had.

'Sorry I'm a bit late.' He was wearing cut-off shorts and a soft, loose T-shirt that had obviously been washed a million times. His jaw was dark with stubble, his eyes were tired, and Kyla thought she'd never seen a sexier man in her life.

'Late? That's a real city-boy remark. I don't think you can be late for a picnic on a beach.' Logan handed him a beer. 'Here. You can drink. I'm on call tonight.'

Ethan took the beer with a nod of thanks. 'I hope you have a better night than I did.'

Logan gave a wry smile and glanced at his daughter. 'I probably won't, actually, but for different reasons. I gather you were up several times.'

'For a small island, they certainly keep you busy,' Ethan drawled, lifting the beer to his lips, and Kyla found herself watching as he drank.

That mouth had been on hers. Those hands had—

Ethan caught her gaze and lowered the beer slowly, his eyes on hers. Neither of them spoke and the tension rose between them until Kyla was aware of nothing but him. She couldn't have looked away if she'd tried, and she sensed that he was experiencing the same inner struggle.

And then Kirsty crawled into her lap and reached for her hair.

'Ow.' The spell broken, Kyla gently prised open Kirsty's chubby fist and removed her hair. 'We need to teach you a new trick.'

To her surprise, Ethan put down his beer and leaned towards Kirsty. 'I'll take her.' He dropped down onto his haunches and smiled at the little girl.

'Fancy a paddle in the waves?'

Kirsty looked uncertain and when Ethan scooped her gently into his arms she went stiff and turned to look at Logan.

'She's a one-man woman,' Logan said smugly, reaching out a hand and smoothing his daughter's silky blonde curls to reassure her, but Ethan spoke softly to the child, pointed to a passing seagull, and Kirsty's face broke into an approving smile.

She forgot her reservations about the tall, dark stranger and with a gurgle of enthusiasm she grabbed a hunk of Ethan's hair in her fist.

'You're in favour, Ethan,' Evanna said cheerfully, reaching for the breadsticks. 'She only pulls the hair out of people she *really* loves.'

Ethan winced and extracted himself from that deadly grip, his dark eyes amused. 'Can I take her to the sea?'

'Of course. She loves it. Did you make any of your peanut chicken, Eva?' Logan leaned forward and studied the picnic, reaching into a bowl and helping himself to a slice of fresh mango. 'This looks delicious.'

'That's Caribbean fruit salad and it's for afterwards.' Evanna pulled the bowl of fruit away from him. 'Leave it alone. You always try and eat my picnics in the wrong order.'

Judging that this would be a good time to leave the two of them alone for a few minutes, Kyla scrambled to her feet and reluctantly followed Ethan towards the sea.

She didn't really want to approach him because then he'd think she hadn't listened to his 'hands-off' message. But she badly wanted to give Logan and Evanna some time on their own.

Frustrated that she suddenly felt so uncomfortable on her own territory, she walked a few paces and then stopped, her attention caught by the scene in front of her.

Ethan had removed Kirsty's shoes and socks and tucked them into the pockets of his shorts. He held her firmly round the waist, dangling her feet gently in the water, dipping her in and out of the breaking waves while she chortled with excitement and kicked her legs.

Kyla smiled at the delight on her niece's face and then found herself looking at Ethan. And couldn't look away. She'd seen him smile before, but not like this. That cool, remote look had gone. Instead, his eyes were gentle and he looked more relaxed than she'd ever seen him.

He lifted Kirsty quickly to avoid a slightly bigger wave, laughing and talking to her quietly, clearly enjoying her company.

He wasn't a man she associated with softness and Kyla watched, transfixed, as the two of them played together, each entertaining the other.

It was only when she tried to swallow that she realised she had a lump in her throat. There was something incredibly moving about watching this strong, reserved man transformed by his interaction with an innocent child.

And then he lifted Kirsty into his arms and she saw something else in his face.

A yearning. And an immense sadness.

Instinctively Kyla moved towards him and then she stopped herself. How could she offer comfort and support when he'd already rejected her? Any gesture like that on her part would be misconstrued. And, anyway, Ethan had already proved on so many occasions that he wasn't a man to open up and confide. What had he ever told her about himself? Hardly anything.

'Kyla!' Evanna's voice came from behind her. 'I've put some food on a plate for you and we're ready to eat.'

Kyla took one last, lingering look at Ethan's broad shoulders and turned away.

She had no idea what was wrong with him but she did know that he wasn't hers to comfort. *He didn't want what she was offering.*

And suddenly she wished she'd never joined them for the picnic.

Maybe, in time, she'd be able to treat Ethan like nothing more than a colleague and friend. Eventually she'd be able to laugh alongside him and enjoy a drink and a casual chat, but she hadn't reached that stage yet. She was painfully aware of him and it was only by a supreme effort of will that she managed not to just sit and stare at him.

Dropping onto her knees on the picnic rug, she reached for the plate. 'Thanks for this. I need to eat quickly and make a move.'

'What's the hurry?' Logan handed her some French bread. 'We've hardly seen you all week and it doesn't get dark for hours. What's the matter with you? You're behaving very oddly.'

'No, I'm not.'

'Well, usually you strip off and swim.'

Usually Ethan wasn't with them.

She just didn't know how to behave in his company any more. If she was chatty and friendly then he'd think that she was trying to flirt with him, and if she ignored him he'd think she was heartbroken. She couldn't win. All she knew was that she needed to put some space between them before she made a fool of herself.

'I have lots to do in the house. I haven't had a chance to tidy up this week.'

Logan frowned at her. 'But you hate tidying up, and—'

'Logan, shut up,' Evanna said gently, interrupting him and pushing a plate of chicken into his hands. 'Stop being so controlling. I'm sure Kyla knows whether she needs an evening at home or not. Why don't you just eat my chicken? Don't let Kirsty grab it—I've done something different for her.'

Kyla mentally blessed Evanna for her tact and then blushed slightly as she felt Logan's searching gaze on her face.

He knew.

She could tell by his face that he knew, and she gave a faint smile and a shrug.

Her brother was very astute about other people's problems, she mused, just not about his own.

When was he going to notice that Evanna was perfect for him?

Ethan returned to the picnic rug and handed Kirsty to Logan. 'She loves the water.'

'Of course. She's a local. She'll swim like a mermaid by the time she's four.' Logan grinned. 'Just like her Aunty Kyla.'

'I was three.'

'And you were always leaping off the rocks into the water. "Keep an eye on your sister Logan."' Logan gave a wry smile as he mimicked his mother's voice. 'You had no sense of danger.'

'You can't live your life looking over your shoulder.' Kyla finished the food on her plate, careful not to look at Ethan. She wanted to swim but not now. Not while he was there. She'd go back to her cottage, wait for them to finish the picnic and then come down later. 'I'm off.' She jumped up and brushed the crumbs from her jeans. 'Thanks, Evanna, that was delicious. Logan, I'll see you tomorrow. Don't forget to phone Mum later. She keeps missing you when she calls and she wants to chat about the arrangements for Aunty Meg's birthday.'

Ethan was watching her. She could *feel* him watching her and she forced herself to cast a casual glance in his direction and smile.

'Bye, Ethan.' She felt as though her face was going to crack. 'See you tomorrow.'

Walk, Kyla, walk. And no looking back.

There are other men out there, she reminded herself as she made her way across the sand to the cottages. Nice men. Uncomplicated ones.

And one day she was going to meet one of them.

CHAPTER SEVEN

ETHAN hesitated by Kyla's back door, knowing that he shouldn't be there. But how could he stay away? She was avoiding her family and he was the cause of it.

She didn't want to bump into him.

Gritting his teeth, Ethan lifted a hand to knock on the door, but at that moment she wandered into the kitchen. And saw him.

She'd obviously just come out of the shower and was wearing a pair of tiny shorts and a skimpy top, and her hair fell in damp, curling waves over her shoulders. Her feet were bare and her legs long and lightly tanned.

Their eyes held for a long moment and he

wondered fleetingly whether she might just
ignore him.

But then she walked over and opened the
door. 'Is something the matter? I was just
going to bed.'

Bed? She looked like that to go to bed?

Ethan felt his blood pressure rise several
notches and suddenly he wished he'd left this
visit until the morning. Everything that needed
to be said could have been said in the harsh light
of day when she was wearing a navy uniform.

Not that her navy uniform did anything to
disguise the tempting curve of her bottom.

'Ethan?' she prompted him with a frown.
'What's the matter?'

He pulled himself together. 'You're going to
bed? It isn't even nine o'clock.'

'I'm tired.'

'Can I come in?'

Something changed in her eyes. Suddenly
they were guarded. Wary. 'Why?'

'Because I need to apologise.' He came

straight to the point, his voice rough. 'And because we need to talk about the other night.'

She didn't play games—*didn't pretend that she didn't know what he was talking about.* She wasn't that sort of woman. 'It was over a week ago, now. It doesn't matter.'

'I've tried pretending that it doesn't matter but it hasn't worked. And it hasn't worked for you either, has it? I haven't seen you at Logan's once this week.' And he knew she was protecting herself.

From him.

She inhaled sharply. 'I've been busy, Ethan.'

'Busy avoiding me.'

Her shoulders stiffened. 'And what if I have? I can read signals. You made your position clear and I'm not a woman who needs to be told anything more than once.'

'What if I told you that you misread the signals?'

'I'd say you were lying.' She tilted her head to one side. 'I know rejection when I see it.'

'No, you don't. That wasn't rejection.'

Suddenly it was imperative that she understood that much at least. 'That wasn't rejection, Kyla.'

'Then my fluency in body language is less accomplished than I thought, because it certainly felt like rejection.'

He didn't associate her with coldness and yet her expression was anything but encouraging. He jabbed his fingers through his hair. 'It wasn't rejection. Far from it. But things are complicated.'

'And I certainly wouldn't want to make them more complicated—goodnight, Ethan.' She made a move to close the door but he stopped her easily and moved inside.

'I'll leave when you've heard me out. There's something I need to tell you. I probably should have told you earlier but I couldn't.'

She hesitated and then let go of the door but she didn't close it. 'All right. I'm listening. You're going to tell me that the kiss was a mistake.'

'It wasn't a mistake. I just didn't plan for it to happen.'

'And do you plan everything that happens in your life?'

'No. But there are things that I need to explain to you before we go any further with this.'

The chemistry was there again, pulsing between them, drawing them in. The wind was blowing outside and yet in her kitchen the air was thick, hot and pulsing with expectation. Suddenly his throat was so dry he could hardly speak and he guessed she was feeling the same way because she swallowed hard.

'You don't have to explain anything to me.'

'Yes.' The dryness made his voice hoarse. 'Yes, I do, Kyla. It's important.'

'Then tell me.'

He almost laughed. *Tell me.* She made it sound so easy and yet now the moment had come he had no idea what to say. He didn't know where to begin. He wasn't even sure where the beginning was.

'Are you married?' Her softly spoken question shocked him.

'Why would you think that?'

'Because I suppose it's the one thing that would stop this thing between us going any further.'

'I'm not married.'

'Then nothing else matters.' She sounded so certain. So confident about everything. And she made life sound simple. 'Ethan, you don't need to worry. Or feel guilty. This isn't right for you and—'

'It's right for me.' He growled the words against her mouth because his hands had reached out and hauled her against him even while his brain had been sending out warnings. He ignored the warnings and kissed her.

Later. He'd worry about everything else later.

Her arms slid round his neck and he felt her slender body press against the hardness of his. He was hot and aroused and more desperate for this woman than he'd been for any other in his life.

He forgot all the reasons why he shouldn't be doing this.

He forgot that she was probably going to hate him when she found out what he was doing there.

He just needed to answer his body's screaming need to possess her in every way.

His hands were on the rounded curve of her bottom when they heard hammering on the door.

Ethan didn't even lift his head but the hammering intensified and she pushed at his chest and he broke the kiss with a fluent curse.

'Yes.' Her flushed cheeks and faint smile told him that she agreed with his assessment of the timing. 'Not good. But I need to see who that is.'

Ethan ran a hand over the back of his neck and hoped that whoever it was could be despatched quickly. 'It's pretty late. Are you expecting anyone?'

'No. But around here people just call. Especially if they're in trouble.' She gave a frown, straightened her top and walked out of the kitchen towards her front door. 'Aisla?'

Ethan heard the surprise in her voice and wondered what on earth Aisla was doing calling so late in the evening with a storm brewing. Was it her diabetes again?

And then she spoke and he heard the raw terror in the woman's voice. 'It's Fraser. He's gone.'

'Gone where?'

'I don't know. He told me he was going to Hamish's for a sleepover but I needed to speak to Hamish's mother about a knitting order, so I rang and she told me that he wasn't with her. And Hamish had no idea where he was.'

Kyla frowned. 'Well, he's an imaginative boy. He's just playing.'

'But it will be dark soon.' Aisla covered her mouth with her hand and shook her head. 'I've told him over and over again that he can't just go off on his own, but he's so independent and he sneaks off when I'm not looking. I'm a terrible mother.'

'You're not a terrible mother,' Kyla said immediately, 'and try not to panic. He's probably gone to tea with someone else and forgotten to phone. Have you called Paul Weston? Henry Mason? They might know.'

'I've called them both and they haven't seen him.'

'Then I'll give Ann Carne a ring,' Kyla said immediately, reaching for the phone. 'She might have an idea what was in his head today.'

Ethan walked forward, ignoring the potential consequences of revealing his presence in Kyla's cottage. 'Where else does he normally play?'

Aisla looked distracted and her eyes were full of fear. 'I don't know—the beach? That's his favourite place. He's always sitting there, dreaming about Vikings and shipwrecks and making up stories in his head.'

Kyla came off the phone. 'Ann Carne said that he was in school until lunchtime and then said he had to go home because he had a doctor's appointment. He gave her a note.'

Aisla stared at her. 'I didn't give him a note.

And Hamish didn't mention that he hadn't been at school this afternoon. Oh, God…'

'There's going to be a perfectly reasonable explanation.' Kyla slipped her feet into the trainers that she'd left lying by the door and reached for a coat from the peg. 'We just need to think logically and not panic. But I think, given the fact that it's going to be dark soon, we should phone Nick Hillier and tell him what's happening. He'll get the whole island searching, if necessary. In the meantime we'll take a look ourselves. I'll go down onto the beach and take a look around.'

Ethan stepped forward, reflecting on the fact that they all turned to Kyla in a crisis. 'I'll just go next door and grab a jacket and my car keys. Then I'll come with you. Two are better than one.'

'Go back to the house,' Kyla told Aisla. 'That way, if he turns up at home, you can let us know. I'll keep my mobile switched on. Call Nick and fill him in.'

Ethan grabbed what he needed from his

cottage and then rejoined Kyla as she walked out of the back door and down onto the beach. Angry streaks were splashed across the darkening sky and the waves lifted and crashed against the rocks at the far end of the bay.

'The storm is closing in. Is it worth calling the coastguard? If Fraser was walking on the cliff path, he could have been swept into the sea.' Ethan stared at the boiling, churning water, trying to not to think about the young boy being devoured by those waves.

'He hasn't been swept into the sea. Don't even think about it.' Kyla spoke briskly but her stride quickened. 'Fraser isn't stupid. And, anyway, we were down there earlier. If he'd been hanging around, we would have seen him.'

'Unless he went to a different beach.'

The both stopped and searched with their eyes and shouted, but their cries were snatched away by the rising wind.

'Why would he go to school for the morning and then leave? It doesn't make sense.' Kyla reached up to stop her hair blowing into her face, a frown in her eyes as she stared at the ocean. 'If you're going to play truant, why turn up at all? Why do half a day at school?'

'You think that's significant?'

'I don't know. It might be. I'm going to call Ann Carne again, but I'll do it from the house. It's too wild on this beach to hear properly. And, Ethan…' She put a hand on his arm and her blue eyes were worried. 'I think you might be right. Perhaps we'd better put in a call to the coastguard. Just put them on alert.'

He followed her to the house and made the call, and when he'd finished she was standing next to him, an urgent look on her face.

'I've spoken to Ann Carne.'

'And?'

'The last lesson of the morning was history. They were doing something on the Celts and Vikings.'

He looked at her blankly, failing to follow her train of thought. 'Why is that significant?'

'Because the bloodiest battle of this island's history was fought between the Celts and the Vikings.'

'And Fraser loves history. It's his favourite subject.' He looked at her, suddenly understanding. 'Where was this battle fought?'

'The castle.'

He gave a grim smile and reached for his keys. 'Let's go.'

Kyla huddled the coat around her and peered at the sky as Ethan pressed his foot to the accelerator. 'There's a wild storm coming. Let's hope we find him before it hits. We could walk from here but it's probably quicker to take the car.'

'He might not be anywhere near the castle. We might be completely wrong. Can we park near the ruins? How close can I get?'

'Pull in further up the road—that's right. This is good. We have to walk from here.' She undid her seat belt and was out of the car before he'd even switched off the engine. 'The kids do come and play up here sometimes. During the day there are guides, waiting to tell horror stories of the dungeons.'

'Just the sort of thing to appeal to a twelve-year-old with a vivid imagination.'

'Precisely.'

'But wouldn't there have been guides today? If he came up here this afternoon then surely someone would have seen him?'

She shook her head. 'It's only open from ten until two. My guess is he actually waited for them to leave so that he could explore.'

'I haven't even had a chance to look round the ruins yet.'

'They're brilliant. Remind me to bring you here under less stressful circumstances.' She broke into a run, thinking about Fraser. What would have been in his head? Where would he have gone?

She clambered over the crumbling stone wall that led into the main part of the castle. 'Fraser? Fraser!' The wind took her voice and carried it away and she looked at Ethan with frustration.

'Even if he is here, he's never going to hear us above the weather.'

'Then we just have to search.'

She looked at him helplessly. 'The place is a warren and it's getting dark.' She suddenly realised that she'd given no thought to the approach of night, and when Ethan pressed a torch into her hand she almost sobbed with relief. 'Thank goodness one of us was thinking.'

'You were thinking, Kyla,' he said roughly, switching on his own torch and sending a powerful beam over the surrounding landscape. 'It was your thinking that got us up here. Now we just need to search. If he's here then he should see the light.'

'Maybe. Maybe not. I've been thinking, Ethan.' Kyla looked round her, focussed her eyes on the dark, crumbling ruins of the castle. 'Fraser wouldn't want his Mum to worry. He wouldn't be hiding on purpose.'

'He played truant.'

'But for the afternoon.' Kyla bit her lip. 'I bet

he was planning to home before the end of school so his mother wouldn't even know he was missing. Don't you remember that day on the beach when he came to get me? He didn't want his mum to know. He really cares about her. He thinks about her.'

'You're suggesting that he's injured.'

'Yes.' Kyla nodded slowly and forced herself to take a deep breath. 'Yes, that's what I think has happened. So he might not see the torch-light, Ethan.'

Ethan's mouth hardened and he gave a nod. 'So we need to look carefully.'

'For goodness' sake, be careful walking along the ramparts. There's a sheer drop on the far side. There is a fence but the wind is fierce.' And she desperately hoped that Fraser hadn't gone in that direction.

Zipping up her coat to give her protection against the rising wind, Kyla moved through the ruins methodically, making the most of her local knowledge to search.

But she saw nothing. Found nothing. And by the time she met up with Ethan again, she was finding it hard not to panic.

'Nothing. No sign of anyone. It was a stupid idea. He obviously isn't here.'

'Well, he's not home either because I just called Nick Hillier to check. I didn't want to worry Aisla, so I called him direct.' The wind howled angrily at them and Ethan caught her arm and drew her behind the comparative shelter of a wall. 'Earlier on, you said something about the guides telling stories about the dungeons.'

'Yes, but you can't go into the dungeons any more because they aren't safe. They've been closed off to the public for years and—' She broke off and shook her head in horror. 'No. No, he wouldn't have done that.'

Ethan closed his hands over the top of her arms and gave her a gentle shake. 'Where's the entrance? Where?'

'You go into the keep and there's a tunnel, but it's blocked off. At the end of the tunnel there's a door, but that's kept locked. There's no way he could—'

'And how do you know about the door, Kyla MacNeil?' He tightened his grip and then released her and started to run towards the keep.

'Because I did the same thing at his age,' Kyla whispered, as she followed him.

CHAPTER EIGHT

THE tunnel was dark and smelt dank and musty.

'At least we can hear ourselves think in here,' Ethan murmured, as he flashed the torch downwards to illuminate their feet. 'I'm beginning to see what you mean about Glenmore and storms.' His feet made a splashing noise and he shone the torch down. 'It's very wet.'

'The rain pours in here. The whole dungeon floods in the winter. Ouch.' She'd lost her footing and clutched at his arm, feeling his muscles bunch under her fingers as he took her weight and steadied her.

'Go slowly. It's treacherous underfoot.'

'Let's try shouting.' She stopped dead. 'Fraser? Fraser!'

Her voice bounced and echoed off the walls and then there was nothing except an eerie silence, punctuated by the sound of water trickling and dripping in the darkness around them.

'This could be a wild-goose chase,' Kyla said, as they picked and slithered their way further down into the tunnel. 'He could be sitting at home and—'

'Be quiet.' Ethan put a hand on her arm. 'I heard something.'

Kyla froze. And then she heard something, too. 'What was that?'

'I don't know. But it wasn't wind and it wasn't dripping water so it's worth investigating. How far is the gate that covers the entrance of the dungeons?'

'I can't remember. It's years since I came down here, but I don't think it can be far now.' Kyla flashed the torch and nodded. 'There. Can you see?'

'Yes. But the gate's shut. It hasn't been opened. Hold the torch while I check.'

Kyla shone both torches onto the gate and Ethan ran his fingers over the rusted bars. 'There's no way he could have got through here.'

'No, but he could have got through there.' Kyla shone the torch to the side and Ethan turned, his eyes on the crack in the wall.

'It's not wide enough.'

'Yes, it is,' Kyla said wearily, and he lifted an eyebrow.

'Are you seriously telling me that you once wriggled through that gap?'

'I was twelve at the time,' she muttered. 'I've eaten thousands of Evanna's dinners since then.'

And then they both heard the noise at the same time. And this time it was recognisable.

'Fraser?' Kyla yelled his name and moved closer to the gate. 'Fraser, is that you? Are you down there?'

'I'm stuck.' His voice was thin and reedy and Kyla felt her heart turn over.

'All right. Don't panic, Fraser. You're going to be fine. We're going to get you out.' She almost laughed as she listened to herself. How? That was the question that flew into her mind. How were they going to get him out? There was a storm brewing, Fraser was trapped underground in an unstable place and no one else knew where they were.

'We need to—we need to—' For once her ingenuity failed her and she looked helplessly at Ethan. 'I don't know what on earth we need. There's a drop, Ethan. He must have fallen in. I mean, there are no stairs or anything. Just a drop and then a small cramped room. It's a bit like being at the bottom of a well. How are we going to get him out of there?'

'A stage at a time.' Ethan was calm. 'First we find a way to get in. Then we find a way to get him out. But we're going to need help. I'm going to go back up to the top and call Nick. We need a team of people up here and some rope. And we need to call the people who run this place to see if there's an official way through this gate.' His quiet confidence gave her courage.

'Yes, of course you're right. Nick will arrange everything if you just call him. I'll stay here and see if I can work anything out.'

'I'll be back in a minute.'

'Kyla?' Fraser's voice came from far below her, weak and shaky. 'Are you still there?'

'I'm still here and I'm not going anywhere. You've chosen a good place to shelter, Fraser, on such a stormy night.'

'It's very dark down here.' She heard the quiver in his voice and her heart twisted with sympathy for him. He must be so scared. For a moment she contemplated dropping the torch down to him but then she realised that the fall would probably just break it and then they'd both be in the dark.

'How did you get down there, Fraser?' She slid a hand across the gate, shuddering when she encountered the softness of a spider's web. She didn't mind the storm or the dark but she hated spiders.

'I opened the gate. I only meant to look. And then I fell. I don't remember anything after that.'

He'd knocked himself out. 'Do you hurt anywhere, Fraser?'

'My head. I think it's bleeding but I dropped my torch when I fell and it broke. I've been lying here. I didn't think anyone would ever find me.'

Kyla closed her eyes for a moment, hardly able to bear thinking about just how frightened he must have felt. 'Well, we *have* found you, and we'll be getting you out in just a moment.' She glanced back up the tunnel and saw the re-assuring flicker of Ethan's torch. He was on his way back. And then she suddenly realised what the child had said. 'You opened the gate? Fraser? Did you say that you opened the gate? How? It's locked.'

'But it opens on the other side. The hinges are rusted.'

'They're on their way.' Ethan stopped next to her and watched while she ran her hands over the gate. 'What are you doing?'

'He didn't go through the gap in the rock. He went through the gate. The gate opens, Ethan.'

She tugged and pulled and the whole structure came towards her. 'Ugh. Spiders. I hate spiders.'

'Kyla?' Fraser's voice came from below them. 'I feel funny.'

'In what way funny?' With Ethan's help, Kyla opened the gate far enough for an adult to pass through. 'Talk to me, Fraser.'

There was a long silence and for a hideous moment she thought he'd lost consciousness. Then his voice came again, this time much weaker. 'Sort of swimmy-headed. And sick. Just not well. I wish I'd never come here now. I want Mum.' The childlike plea for protection went straight to Kyla's heart but before she could act, Ethan moved her bodily and handed her his torch.

'Hold on, Fraser.' His voice was deep and re-assuring. 'I'm coming down to you.'

'You can't do that.' Kyla caught his arm but he shrugged her off.

'I have to. We don't know what his injuries are. He's afraid and on his own. Someone needs to be down there with him.'

'You can't just jump, Ethan. It's too far. You'll break something.'

'I'm not jumping.' He removed his coat. 'There are enough handholds in this place to climb down.'

'Are you kidding?' She eyed him with incredulity. 'The wall is completely smooth.'

'No, it isn't. Stay there for a moment and then hand me the torch when I say so. Fraser?' He raised his voice and wriggled his body through the gap in the gate. 'I'm coming down to you. Just hang on.'

There was no answer, only the hollow plop of water, and suddenly Kyla felt sick herself. She ought to stop Ethan doing something so rash but she knew now that Fraser's life could be at stake. Why wasn't he answering? Was he unconscious?

Ethan gave a grunt as he anchored himself and held out a hand. 'Hand me the torch.'

'But you won't have any hands to hold on, and—'

'The torch, Kyla!'

'All right.' She bit back the impulse the tell him to be careful. They were all way past the point of being careful.

He took the torch in his mouth and started to descend with a smooth agility that astonished her.

And then she remembered the way he ran in the mornings. He may have been brought up in a city, but there was no doubting his physical fitness. Still, physical fitness was one thing. Climbing down a wall into a long abandoned dungeon was quite another.

Fifteen minutes, Kyla calculated, feeling the thump of her heart and the dampness of her palms. That was how long it would take Nick and a rescue team to reach them. Would that be fifteen minutes too long for Fraser?

They had no idea about the extent of his injuries.

All they knew now was that he wasn't responding to their questions.

She didn't dare flash the torch in case she distracted Ethan from his task. Instead she sat and forced herself to breathe steadily, braced to hear the sound of his powerful body crashing to the ground.

'I'm down, Kyla.' His voice echoed up to her from the bowels of the dungeon. 'Can you shine some extra light down here? It's pitch dark.'

She did as he'd asked, hugely relieved that he'd made it that far without injury to himself. And then she heard noise from above her and realised that the rescue party had arrived. 'They're here, Ethan. Have you found him? Is Fraser OK?' Suddenly she wished she'd been the one to go down the shaft. She felt so helpless, just sitting at the top. If she hadn't been holding the torch, she would have bitten her nails down to the quick.

'He has a nasty laceration to his forehead and some bruising, but I don't think anything is broken. He's OK. Conscious. Just a bit weak.'

And extremely frightened, Kyla was willing to bet. She could hear Ethan talking to the boy and then there was a crunch of footsteps behind her and she turned to see Logan standing there, along with Nick and two other members of the coastguard.

'We've brought ropes, and there's more equipment up top.' A light shone from the helmet on Nick's head. 'Give us an update.'

'Ethan is down there so it shouldn't be too hard to get him out,' Kyla said, moving onto her hands and knees so that she could get a better look over the edge. 'Ethan?'

'Drop a harness on a rope?' Logan turned to Ben. 'We can bring him up that way.'

Ben nodded agreement. 'That will certainly be the quickest way if the boy is up to it. Is he conscious?'

'Yes, I think so.' Kyla supplied the information they needed, and Ben frowned.

'How the hell did Ethan get down there?'

'He climbed down.' And Kyla was still wondering how a man who dressed in suits costing thousands of pounds could so skilfully negotiate a sheer and slippery face.

'Without a rope?'

Kyla heard the disapproval in Ben's voice and threw him an impatient glance. 'Fraser stopped talking. We were worried about him. If you were the one sitting here, would you have waited for a rope?'

'Probably not.' Ben gave a faint smile of apology. 'Good decision, then. Brave guy. That's another free pint I owe him. All right. Let's get on with this. The weather's getting worse and if he needs a lift to the mainland, it's going to have to be soon.'

Logan was shouting down to Ethan, trying to assess the medical situation and how best to extract Fraser. 'I still think the best way is to drop a harness. He's conscious and Ethan has dressed the wound on his head. He can use his feet to keep away from the side. We'll have him out in minutes that way.'

'Let's do it.'

After that everything happened quickly. They lowered the rope to Ethan and minutes later Kyla saw the top of Fraser's head appear over the lip of the dungeon. She breathed a sigh of relief and suddenly realised that her hands were shaking.

She'd been so afraid for him.

His face was streaked with dirt and blood and although he had a sheepish smile on his face, she sensed that he was struggling with tears.

Logan lifted him clear of the gate and sat him carefully down on the damp floor of the tunnel.

'You are such a brave boy.' Kyla took one look at him and wrapped her arms around him. 'If the Celts had had you on their side, those Vikings never would have stood a chance.' She could feel him quivering and cuddled him close.

His teeth were chattering. 'My mum's going to kill me.'

Ben nodded as he slipped some warm layers over the boy. 'Very probably. But then she'll be relieved you're OK. He's bleeding through that pad. Logan? Kyla?'

'I've got it.' Kyla gently lifted the pad on the boy's forehead and studied the wound under the torchlight. She could see that it was deep and the edges were jagged. 'I'll put a firm dressing on it for now just so that we can get you out of here, Fraser. Then one of the doctors is going to take a closer look at that.' It was obvious to her that he was going to need stitches and she glanced towards Logan, who gave a swift nod of understanding.

'I want you to answer a couple of questions for me, Fraser,' he said casually, shining a light into the boy's eyes to check the reaction of his pupils. 'What day is it today?'

Fraser answered correctly and Logan slipped the penlight back into his pocket.

'What's your mum's name?'

'Aisla. And she's definitely going to kill me.'

Logan grinned. 'I'll protect you. How's the headache?'

'Better than it was.'

'Do you feel sick?'

Fraser shook his head and at that moment Ethan joined them. 'He thinks he lost consciousness when he fell, but his GCS was fifteen when I checked it down there.'

Kyla looked at them. 'Will you transfer him to the mainland for a CT scan?'

'I wouldn't go down that route yet,' Ethan said easily, glancing towards Logan. 'It's true that he was knocked out, but he's not showing any clinical signs of a skull fracture. I'd suggest we just observe him and see how he goes.'

Logan nodded agreement. 'Let's get him to the surgery,' he said quietly, 'and then we can take a proper look at him under some decent lights. I'll stitch him up, check him out and then see what's needed. He can stay the night with me and then I can watch him.'

'Is Evanna with you?' Kyla was still holding Fraser and her brother nodded.

'Yes. She came over to stay with Kirsty when I got the call about Fraser. So she can keep an eye on him, too.' He put a hand on Fraser's shoulder and squeezed. 'You're going to have plenty of attention.'

'Will Nurse Duncan make one of her cakes? I've been down here since lunchtime and I'm *starving*.'

Logan looked amused. 'At this time of night? I doubt it. But I expect she'll whip you up something good to eat if you play your cards right.'

Kyla looked at Ethan. 'You never told me you could climb.'

'You never asked.'

Was it all about questions for him? 'You never reveal anything about yourself unless it's prised out of you?'

He wiped the mud from his cheek with the sleeve of his jacket. 'I'm not much of a talker, you know that.' He reached out a hand and touched Fraser's head. 'You did well. How are you feeling now?'

'OK.' Fraser looked at him and something passed between them. An understanding. 'Thanks.'

'You're welcome,' Ethan said, a glimmer of a smile touching his usually serious face.

Logan looked at Kyla and then back at Ethan. 'You two are filthy. Anyone would think you'd spent the evening scrabbling around in a dark tunnel. You're a bad advert for the surgery. I'm the one on call so go home and have a shower. I'll take over here but keep your phone switched on. If I need you, I'll call.'

The storm struck at dawn.

Hearing a consistent hammering, Ethan woke from a restless sleep, wondering whether the wind was rattling the windows. Then he realised that the hammering was coming from the back door.

Trouble with Fraser?

He'd rung Logan before going to bed and his colleague had assured him that Fraser was sleeping and seemed comfortable. He'd been sick once but that was to be expected after a head injury and Logan hadn't been unduly concerned. All his other signs were fine and they had been going to monitor him.

The hammering came again, louder this time, and Ethan forced himself out of bed.

Wondering what new crisis he was about to face, he tugged on a pair of jeans, jerked open the door and felt his entire body tense.

Kyla stood there, her face alight with excitement. 'Come with me. There's something I want to show you.'

Ethan pushed away the claws of sleep that were threatening to drag him down. 'Something's happened to Fraser? He was OK when I rang.'

'As far as I know, he's still OK. This isn't about Fraser. It's nothing to do with work.' She held out a hand. 'Come with me.'

'Now?'

She smiled. 'Now is the best time.'

'It's the middle of the night. There's a storm building. It's wild outside.'

'It hasn't even begun yet, and it's dawn. There's plenty of light.' There was a strange gleam in her eyes. 'Are you afraid, Ethan?'

Everything about her seemed vivid and full of life, and Ethan realised that the answer to her question should be yes. He was afraid.

But not of the storm. He was afraid of her. Of his feelings for her. Of where this wild, crazy chemistry was going to take them.

He still hadn't told her the truth about himself.

'There won't be anything to see in this weather. It's raining and the visibility is zero.'

'Now you're talking like an Englishman.' She thrust his coat into his hands and opened the front door. The wind tried to slam it shut again but Kyla leaned against it with her shoulders and zipped up her jacket. 'I hope you're feeling fit, Ethan.'

'Where are we going?' They were outside now and he had to shout to make himself heard above the screaming, howling wind. It slammed into them as they left the cottage, as if fiercely angry that anyone should dare to venture into its territory.

'Back up to the castle. Only this time we're walking.'

'Sorry?' He shot her an incredulous look, wondering what had happened to her. 'Kyla, we just came from there.'

'This is different. You said that you hadn't seen the ruins.'

'There's a storm and it's not even fully light yet.'

'It's the best time. Trust me.'

This time she ignored the car and crossed the road towards the grassy hill that led to the ruins, her hair blowing across her face.

The jagged outline of the castle was barely visible through the driving rain, and Ethan grimaced and wiped the water from his eyes as the spray of the sea mixed with the rain. He tasted salt, felt the air sting his cheeks and looked at Kyla in disbelief.

Being out in this weather was crazy, but she didn't seem to see anything odd in it.

The rain had turned her soft honey-coloured hair to sleek, dark gold and droplets of water clung to her lashes and her cheeks, but she didn't seem to care. In fact, he would have said that she relished being so close to the elements. He'd never seen her happier.

And her response intrigued him because he knew no other woman who would have been so comfortable in such filthy weather conditions.

She was half-wild, he thought to himself, watching as she scrambled over a gate and started up the grassy slope. The wind crashed across her path, trying to turn her, but she was graceful and sure-footed as she ran, and Ethan could do nothing but follow, exhilaration mingling with exasperation.

She scrambled over the outer walls of the castle that were now no more than a few ruined rocks, and climbed across some uneven ground that led to the ancient, crumbling fort.

'We have to climb up.' She raised her voice to be heard above the wind and he followed her and then stopped, suddenly understanding why she'd brought him here.

Furious red streaks were splashed across the sky, as if an artist had just taken a brush and angrily thrown paint at a canvas. The grey, threatening outline of the ruins loomed from the rain and mist and beyond that stretched the sea, boiling and foaming with fury as the wind and the currents fought for supremacy.

'You can imagine it, can't you? The Vikings landing there?' She steadied herself, pointed down to the beach, and then lifted her hand to anchor her hair, which was blowing wildly. With a shift of her feet she balanced herself against the wind as she stared across the west of the island. 'They must have looked up and seen this castle and been afraid. They must have wondered whether to turn home and give up. When I stand up here in a storm I can feel the history of the place so strongly.'

He couldn't take his eyes off her profile. 'You're as bad as Fraser.'

'There's nothing wrong with being interested in your heritage.' She turned to face him and smiled. 'Was it worth the climb?'

He dragged his eyes away from her and stared

at the ruins and then at the sea. He'd never seen a wilder, more atmospheric place. 'It was worth the climb.'

'This place is at its best when the weather is bad.'

He laughed and shook his head. 'You're crazy, do you know that?'

'Am I?' The wind gusted and she grabbed his arm for support. 'If we drop down to just below the ruined tower, it's sheltered. We can sit there and watch the sun come up.'

Ethan stared at the sky. 'I don't think there's going to be any sun,' he muttered, but he followed her across the patch of grass, over some stones and down again until they were sheltered by a large wall.

'Do you have any idea how old this place is? They reckon it's one of the earliest castles, although it's been built on over the centuries, of course.' She ran her hands over the grey, uneven bricks and looked through the tiny slit window. 'When I was a child I used to come up here with Logan and play warriors. He used to be the invading army and I used to be the one defending the castle.'

He could imagine her doing exactly that, with her hair streaming down her back, her chin lifted and her eyes blazing as she and Logan argued over who was in charge.

'Did you cover him in boiling oil?'

'No. Buckets of ice-cold water. My aim was brilliant. He used to complain like mad.' She stepped towards him and took the front of his jacket in her hands. 'You were brave last night with Fraser. You acted like an islander.'

Her face was so close that her cheek almost brushed against his. Ethan clenched his jaw and kept his eyes ahead because he knew that to look at her now would be too great a test of his self-control. And then she moved her head fractionally and he felt her touch her lips to his, and he just couldn't help himself. He was drawn to her in the same way that he'd been drawn to her on that very first day. He looked. And fell. Deep,

deep into her stormy blue eyes that held both warning and invitation.

He issued his own warning. 'I'm not an islander.' There was so much that he still had to tell her and yet suddenly he couldn't remember any of it with the heat and awareness devouring them both like a greedy animal.

Her mouth was so close to his that he could feel her breath mingling with his. 'But you could be, Ethan. You could be.'

He was surrounded by her. The scent of her. The sound of her. The feel of her. His insides locked with lust. And in those tense, sexually charged few moments they both knew what was going to happen.

He was seeing it in her eyes and he knew that she was seeing it in his. And suddenly all the reasons that he shouldn't be doing this were eclipsed by all the reasons that he should.

He lifted his hand and cupped the back of her head, drawing her face towards his. 'It's got to be here,' he growled hoarsely, 'and now.' He

was driven by an urgency that he didn't understand and she obviously felt it, too, because she
pressed closer and lifted her face.

'Yes. Now.' She met the hot burn of his kiss and
struggled with the zip of his coat just as he
reached for her clothes. There was no gentle
fumbling. No smiles or laughter. Each was deadly
serious, intent on the other, eyes clinging and
hands brushing in a feverish determination to
discover flesh and be together. His mouth still on
hers, he stripped her of her coat and then grabbed
the hem of her strap top and slid it upwards.

She lifted her arms in acquiescence and he
broke the kiss just long enough to jerk the top
over her head. He looked, just for a moment—
saw high, firm breasts and nipples darkening to
a peak—and then looking just wasn't enough
and he touched.

This time his hands were on bare, warm flesh
and he held her against him, feeling the perfection of her slender body against his.

'Ethan…Ethan…' She murmured his name

against his lips, pressing forward, boldly encouraging him. He felt her quiver under his hands—felt her skin sleek and soft as his fingers explored and discovered. She gasped against the relentless assault of his mouth and then he felt the scratch of her nails over the bare flesh of his chest and the nip of her teeth on his jaw. Only then did he realise that she'd ripped at his clothes with the same feverish desperation that he'd stripped her. His shirt hung open and her hands were on his chest.

And then she kissed and nipped and licked her way from his jaw to his neck and from his neck to his chest, touching, tasting and breathing in the scent of him until he was so aroused that his body ached with it.

And when he felt her fingers on the waistband of his jeans he sucked in a breath and clamped his hands over hers, his teeth gritted.

'Wait.' He held her away from him, struggling to find a control that had never eluded him before. 'You have to wait.'

'I can't wait. And neither can you.' She was on her toes, seeking his mouth with hers. 'Why wait?'

'Because I want you so badly.'

'That's the way I want you to want me, Ethan. What other way is there?' Her voice soft, she moved her face against his and he felt the soft brush of her lashes against his cheek before her mouth found his again. Her tongue teased his lower lip and then the corner of his mouth, accelerating the excitement between them to such a pitch that the very idea of control became laughable.

His mind and vision blurred, Ethan dispensed with the barrier of her shorts and panties and slid his hands down over her bottom. And this time when he felt her fingers at his zip, he didn't stop her but neither did he hesitate in his own quest to know all of her. He slid his fingers deep inside her and she was so wet and so hot that he cursed softly and buried his face in her neck.

'Now, Ethan.' She was almost sobbing as she

freed him from his jeans and closed her hand around him. 'Please, now.'

And afterwards when he thought about this moment, he realised that he'd never really had a choice.

From that first moment on the ferry, this had been inevitable. Not here, perhaps, and not in this way. This frantic, greedy, desperate coupling that was almost primitive in its intensity. But it had always been there, waiting for both of them.

And when he pushed her back against the ancient stone wall and lifted her, he wondered how many other such acts of such sensual desperation this castle had seen over the centuries.

And then thinking became impossible because it was all about feeling and acting on the most basic of human instincts. She wrapped her legs around his waist and he moved his hand down and guided himself into her tight, silken heat, driven by a devouring, dangerous force beyond his control. His need was primitive and he deepened his possession, his hands supporting her as he held her still for his most intimate invasion. Dimly he registered her cry and tried to pause, wondering whether he'd hurt her, and then he felt the frantic movement of her hips, encouraging him, and gave himself up to his body's instinctive need to thrust into her.

The fire between them burned and licked as they moved and gasped and greedily devoured each other. And then the explosion came. Powerful and deadly, it took both of them with it and Ethan ground into her one last time, driven past control by the rhythmic contractions of her own body.

And then the storm left, as if satisfied that it had done its work.

Still breathing heavily, Ethan lowered her gently to the ground and tried to clear his head, still too stunned to form a coherent sentence. Would he ever be able to speak?

What was there to say? After sharing something so perfect, what was there to say?

She was shaking in his arms, her hair tangled and loose, her body deliciously naked.

And suddenly he wanted her again. And he knew that he'd want her again after that. And again.

He cupped her face in his hands, needing to communicate the way he felt but silenced by his natural reticence. 'Kyla—'

'Don't say anything,' she said shakily, her eyes shy as she looked at him. 'Don't say anything at all.'

And he knew that she understood and felt the same way.

There were no words that could possibly do justice to what they'd just shared.

He gently stroked her hair away from her face, noticing things that he'd never noticed before. Like the fact that her blue eyes were darker than he'd first thought and she had a few tiny freckles over her nose. He dragged his thumb slowly over her full mouth and she nipped at it, the look in her eyes reflecting his own thoughts.

He wanted her again.

But not here.

'The sun is coming up.' He spoke softly, even though there was no one around to hear them. 'The storm is over.'

'Let's watch. I'll show you where.' She stooped and retrieved her clothes, dressing quickly in a series of graceful movements that he watched with masculine hunger. Then she reached forward and started to fasten the buttons on his shirt. 'If I don't do this, I won't be able to leave you alone. I love your body—have I told you that?'

No. And he hadn't told her that he loved hers, although their frantic love-making should surely have left her in no doubt. But her observation that intimate conversations hadn't been part of their interaction to date was a sharp, uncomfortable reminder that this relationship was built on shaky, dangerous ground.

She took his hand and led him across a low stone wall and then sank to the grass and dragged him down next to her. 'This is the best view on the whole island. And this is the best weather in which to see it. Just watch.'

Ethan sat, silenced by the beauty of the scene unfolding in front of him. And as he sat there, watching the sun come up over an angry, boiling sea, he suddenly understood.

Kyla reached for his hand and curled her fingers around his. 'Do you think things happen for a reason, Ethan?'

'What do you mean?'

Perhaps she heard the wariness in his voice because she smiled. 'I mean that some things are just meant to happen. You came out of nowhere. Serendipity. You could have chosen to escape anywhere but you came here.'

Ethan felt coldness pour through his body.

It hadn't been serendipity.

And he hadn't come out of nowhere.

Her words were like a hammer blow to his conscience and the perfection of the moment was soured. 'Kyla—'

She covered his lips with her finger, preventing him from finishing his sentence. 'Not now. Now I just want you to kiss me again. And then we'll go home and do everything again in slow motion.'

CHAPTER NINE

UNFORTUNATELY, fate intervened in the form of a little girl with an asthma attack.

Logan was still tied up with Fraser, who was now being sick and complaining of persistent headache, so Ethan had no choice but to leave Kyla on her doorstep.

Once again he seemed distant, remote and Kyla felt a twist of yearning for the unconstrained, passionate side of him she'd discovered up in the ruins of the castle.

For a moment he'd lost control and finally revealed himself to her but now he had retreated back into his shell.

'I'll see the Roberts child, come back here and change and then go straight to the surgery.

Logan thinks he may have to fly Fraser over to the mainland for a CT scan.'

They might have been no more than colleagues, discussing their plans for the day. Visit here. Clinic there.

Where had it gone? Kyla wondered as she stared wistfully into his handsome face—that incredible closeness and intimacy that had held them both in its grip. *Where had it gone?*

'On second thoughts, would you mind picking up a suit for me?' He handed her his keys. 'I can take a shower at Logan's and change before surgery. It will be quicker than coming all the way back here.'

'Of course.' She took the keys and waited for him to say something that indicated he understood the way she was feeling. *Something that acknowledged the power of what they'd shared during the storm.* But he didn't even look at her.

His handsome face was grim and serious as if he had a thousand things on his mind and none of them related to her.

'That's fine.' She forced herself to speak normally and not show her disappointment. 'I'll bring the suit. Will I be able to find it?'

'In the wardrobe in my bedroom. Just choose one. And Kyla…' Finally he looked at her but there was a bleakness in his eyes that did nothing to alleviate the growing ache inside her. 'This evening, we have to talk.'

Talk? She watched him stride towards his car, the lump in her throat as big as the weight in her heart.

She loved him, she realised with a sinking feeling. Somehow, over the past weeks, she'd grown to love this complicated man. And up until five minutes ago she would have sworn that he had feelings for her, too.

Had she imagined what they'd shared in the castle?

No. She definitely hadn't. She was just being paranoid, she told herself as she turned and let herself into her own house. She'd shower and change and then collect his suit on her way to work.

She had nothing to worry about.

The fact that he was suddenly serious and detached was just Ethan being Ethan. He was thinking about work. That was what he did.

As she stripped off her clothes she was suddenly deliciously aware of the unfamiliar ache in various parts of her body and a soft smile touched her mouth. He felt something for her, of course he did. How, otherwise, could he have made love to her in the way that he had? She just had to be patient and allow him the space he obviously needed.

He wasn't a man who opened up easily, she knew that.

She dried her hair, dressed in her uniform and picked up his keys.

Inside his cottage, she sprinted up the stairs, found the suit and carried it out of the house. It was only as she went to hang it in the rear of her car that she saw the letter that had dropped out of the pocket onto the road.

With a frown, she picked it up, intending to push it back into the suit pocket. And then a sentence caught her eye and she froze in shock. And started to read.

'So are you going to transfer Fraser to the mainland for a CT scan?' Ethan asked the question as Logan reached for the telephone.

'Yes. I'm pretty sure he's just displaying signs of concussion but I need to be sure. It's best to play it safe because I don't want any last-minute emergencies.' He broke off as the door crashed open and Kyla strode into the reception area. 'Oops. My sister obviously climbed out of bed on the wrong side.'

Ethan felt himself tense as she kicked the door shut behind her, dropped her bag by the reception desk and blew a strand of hair out of her eyes.

Then she looked at him.

And he saw that she knew.

There was contempt in her eyes as she stalked over to him and thrust the suit into his hands, her face unsmiling. 'Your suit, Dr Walker. Better put it on quickly. It's part of your disguise.'

Logan gave her an incredulous look. 'Are you hormonal?'

She whirled on her brother, anger sparking in her blue eyes. 'No. I am *not* hormonal.'

'Then what the hell is wrong with you?'

'You'd better direct that question to Dr Walker,' she suggested in an acid tone, and Ethan inhaled sharply.

'Kyla, why don't we go somewhere quiet and talk?'

'Don't you mean somewhere quiet so that we can carry on keeping our secrets? Or rather *your* secrets.' Her gaze was accusing. 'And what do you mean, *talk?* Since when did you ever talk, Ethan? You're more of a listener, aren't you? Especially when you're finding out about people.'

Wishing he hadn't taken so long to tell her the truth, Ethan watched her steadily. She was a woman of wild extremes. Whatever Kyla did, she did it with an abandoned passion. She made love as though she was enjoying her last moments on earth and she lost her temper with the same degree of intensity. With Kyla, there was no neutral. No grey areas.

So how on earth was he going to explain himself to her? Especially when he couldn't even explain things to himself.

'Surgery is about to start,' Logan pointed out in a quiet tone, 'so whatever it is that's bugging the pair of you, you need to shelve it until later. There's enough gossip on this island without adding more.'

Kyla turned to him. 'Ethan is—'

'I don't want to hear it, Kyla.' Logan's voice was firm. 'Get set up for clinic. We'll talk later. And now I need to sort out Fraser.'

Kyla hesitated and it was obvious that she was struggling with her emotions. Then she blinked several times, swallowed hard and walked towards her room with her head down.

'Women,' Logan said wearily, watching her

go. 'Don't you ever wish they came with an instruction manual?'

Kyla buried herself in her clinic but her mind wouldn't focus. She didn't know whether to cry or punch something and in the end she just did everything on automatic. She took blood pressures, she talked about asthma management, she syringed an ear, took a cervical smear and changed two dressings. Then she realised that she hadn't even noticed what the wounds underneath had looked like.

All she'd been thinking about was Ethan.

And the letter.

She gave up and went next door to Evanna.

'I'm sorry to ask you this.' Her voice was gruff. 'But have you got time to finish my clinic? I've only got three more to see but I'm not concentrating. I think I need some air before I put a dressing on someone who needs an ECG.'

Evanna put down the tourniquet she was holding. 'Of course. What's the matter? Are you ill? Perhaps it was being stuck in that dark tunnel in the storm.'

'I'm not ill,' Kyla assured her dully, backing towards the door. 'I just feel a bit— I need to—'

'It's OK,' Evanna said in a soft voice, waving a hand at her. 'Just go. You don't need to explain.'

Kyla gave her a grateful smile and slid out of the room just as Ethan emerged from his.

They looked at each other and then she sucked in a breath and made for the car park.

'Kyla, wait.' His voice was a firm command but she ignored him and lengthened her stride. He'd had plenty of opportunity to talk to her and he hadn't bothered. And she certainly wasn't ready to talk to *him*. Maybe she wouldn't ever be ready. She felt completely betrayed.

She climbed into her car and sped away, determined to find herself somewhere peaceful to think.

Instinctively she headed for the ruined castle and then wished she hadn't because the place was now layered with memories of Ethan and it was impossible to think clearly with thoughts of earlier intruding.

There was no trace of the storm now and the sun shone in a perfectly blue sky, but still Kyla shivered as she sank down onto a rock and stared bleakly out to sea.

And then she heard a firm, masculine tread behind her and she rose to her feet, accusation in her eyes because she knew who it would be. And perhaps, secretly, she'd wanted him to follow her so that they could say what needed to be said, in privacy.

'Why did you follow me?'

'Because we need to talk and we don't need to do it in public.' He stopped a little distance away from her and she turned away, ignoring the wisps of hair that blew across her face.

'You mean that you don't want anyone else to hear your secret.'

'I don't want them to hear it yet.' His voice was even. Steady. 'First, you and I need to talk.'

'Why?' She turned back to face him, so angry

that she clenched her hands into fists. 'So that you can make excuses?'

'I'm not going to make excuses.'

How could he be so calm? 'You deceived us, Ethan.' Her voice broke and she hated herself for showing just how badly his betrayal had hurt her. 'You deceived us all. Not just me but Logan, Evanna—the whole island. We thought—we thought you were—'

'You thought I was Ethan Walker, and that's exactly who I am.'

She looked him full in the face, not giving him room for escape. 'But you're also Catherine's brother,' she said in a whisper. *'Catherine's brother.'*

He stepped towards her. 'Kyla—'

'You're not a stranger. It wasn't serendipity that brought you here. You came here for a reason. You came to find her child, didn't you? You came for your niece. *You came after Kirsty.*'

Tension stiffened his shoulders. 'I wanted to meet her, yes.'

'No, Ethan.' Kyla shook her head and hugged her arms around her waist. 'Wanting to meet her would have been you walking off that ferry and saying, "Hi, I'm Kirsty's uncle." And you didn't do that. You stayed on the edges and watched. You ate our food and you drank our drink. You listened to our conversations and lived our lives with us, *and all the time you were just watching.*'

'There were things I needed to understand. I wanted to get to know you all.'

'And is that your excuse for making love to me? Did you need a few extra intimate details for your research?' She forced herself to say the words—forced herself to stare hurt in the face. 'I suppose that's the ultimate way of getting to know someone, isn't it? What are you going to do next? Move on to Evanna just to check that you know her, too?'

'Don't, Kyla—'

'Don't what? Don't face up to facts? I'm being honest, which is more than you've been up until now.'

His shoulders were tense. 'What happened between us had absolutely nothing to do with the fact that I'm Catherine's brother.'

'Yes, it did, because you wouldn't even have *been* here if you hadn't been Catherine's brother! We would never have met. You deliberately hid your identity from me. From all of us.'

'I tried to tell you.'

'But you didn't try hard enough, did you? What were you thinking?' The lump in her throat threatened to choke her and the anger burned inside her. 'Were you checking out whether Logan was a fit enough father? Because I can tell you now that he's worth six of you. Logan is honest and straightforward, and if you are thinking of doing *anything* that will hurt my brother or his child, I will personally see you off this island.' Breathless, she stopped, her chest rising and falling as she struggled for control.

A muscle worked in his lean cheek, an indication of his own rising tension. 'You want me to explain so let's start with that. You feel protective of Logan. You love him.'

'Of course I love him.' Her tone was both dismissive and impatient because she couldn't understand why he was wasting time stating the obvious. 'He's my brother. He's family.'

'You make it all sound so straightforward, but life isn't always like that, Kyla. It's complicated.'

'What's complicated about telling the truth? You should have just told us. That's what I would have done.'

Ethan swore softly and closed the distance between them. 'Maybe it is, but I'm not like you and my family is nothing like yours.'

Kyla tried to step backwards but he caught her shoulders and forced her to look at him.

'You want to talk about this? All right, let's talk about it.' His voice was raw with a depth of emotion that she hadn't heard from him before. 'Your family is a single unit. You're in and out of each other's lives, interfering and interacting. You're individuals but you're all small parts of a whole.'

She ignored the fact that his fingers were digging into her shoulders. 'So? That's what families are.'

'Not mine.' He released her then and his hands dropped to his sides, his tone hoarse. 'Not mine, Kyla.'

'I know your parents were divorced and re-married, but—'

'You don't know anything.' He stared out across the sea. 'Catherine and I didn't share the same brother-sister relationship that you have with Logan. You love Logan. Do you want to know how I felt about Catherine? For most of my life, I hated her. There.' He turned to look at her, a smile of self-derision on his handsome face. 'Now are you shocked?'

She didn't know what to say so she didn't say anything, and he turned away again with a humourless laugh.

'Oh, yes, you're shocked, because hating your

family isn't something that really happens around here, is it, Kyla? Around here, on Glenmore, family is the most important thing. But the truth is that I hated Catherine. And she hated me, too. From the moment we met when I was eleven and she was eight, we hated each other. She hated me because my father married her mother and she liked it being just the two of them. It meant that she had to compete for attention. I hated her because she was the most selfish person I had ever met. She believed that the whole world had to revolve around her and it drove me mad. She took drugs, she stole, she did just about anything a person can do to gain attention. And I hated her.'

Reminding herself that he'd deceived her, Kyla tried to hold onto her anger but she felt it slipping out of her. 'You were a child.'

'Don't make excuses for me. Catherine and I spent the next ten years trying to make each other miserable, and usually succeeding. We argued, we fought, we each blamed the other for our terrible home life. She was half-wild, always running away from school and driving my father mad. Three times he had to collect her from the police station—did she ever tell you that? I thought she was incredibly selfish. She thought I was aloof, remote and judgmental. We couldn't wait to get out of each other's lives.'

'When did you last see her?'

'Ten years ago.'

'Ten years…' Kyla tried to imagine not seeing Logan for ten years. 'So—why did you follow her here? Why now if you didn't have that sort of relationship?'

For a long moment Ethan didn't answer. 'She wrote to me, a year ago, and I realise now that it was probably just a few days before she went into labour with Kirsty. It was the only letter I ever had from her and probably the only communication we had that wasn't tinged with bitterness. She wrote because she said that she'd discovered paradise. She told me that she'd settled in Scotland and suddenly felt different about life. She realised that family were important and she wanted to make contact. She told me that I was going to be an uncle.'

'Did you write back?'

'By the time I received her letter, she was already dead.'

'But—'

'I was working in the Sudan, Kyla. I was in Africa. I was battling heat and dust and disease like you cannot possibly imagine.' His voice was raw and she suddenly realised just how much of this man she didn't know. She'd assumed he'd worked in London. 'She sent the letter to my flat in London. For some reason it wasn't forwarded. I only received it two months ago when I finally came home.'

'So why not just turn up here and introduce yourself? Why pretend to be someone else?'

He frowned in response to her question. 'I didn't pretend.'

'But her surname was King. How can you be Walker?'

'Her mother refused to take my father's name. She was always King and I was Walker.'

'She never mentioned you,' Kyla told him. 'She always said that her family could have done with living on Glenmore for a while. I suppose she felt that having the baby was a time to make a fresh start.'

'That letter has tortured me. It left me with so many unanswered questions. The Catherine in that letter bore no resemblance to the Catherine of my childhood. She claimed it was this place that had changed her.' He breathed in and looked around him. 'She said that it was Glenmore. The sea, the ruins, the wildness. And most of all the people.'

'She arrived on the ferry one day with a backpack and never left. Glenmore has that effect on some people.' *But not on him.* The island hadn't changed him or caused him to open up to others. He was as reserved and self-contained as ever.

'Something in her letter affected me deeply.

She described everything in such detail. Not just the scenery but the people. She talked about everyone as if she knew them. It was the first time I'd ever had the sense that she had been interested in anything other than herself. That letter showed me a completely different side of her.'

'She fitted in very quickly.' Kyla watched his face, trying to gauge his reaction, but as usual he gave nothing away. 'So what made you come here? Was it just Kirsty?'

'No. I felt as though I'd lost something. Which was ridiculous because up until that letter Catherine and I had never had anything that we could lose. We'd never shared anything. But she'd obviously discovered a different part of herself and new priorities. And maybe I had, too.' He gave a faint smile. 'A year working in Africa does tend to sort out your priorities. Her letter was intriguing. I suppose I wanted to see the place that had changed her so dramatically. I wanted to see Glenmore the way she would have seen it. And, of course, I wanted to meet my niece and the man who my sister fell in love with and married.'

'And you couldn't just have been honest with us?' Despite what he'd told her, she was still angry with him. *Angry that he hadn't told her the truth.* 'Couldn't you have told *me?*' Her implication was clear, and he didn't flinch from her gaze.

'I'm used to doing things by myself. I'm used to finding my own way. That's the person I am, Kyla.'

She refused to let him duck the issue. 'You deceived us.'

'Not intentionally and not in the way that you mean. I was always going to tell you. I'm just sorry you found out in the way you did.'

'The letter fell out of your pocket. I didn't intend to read it but then I saw Kirsty's name.' She took a deep breath. 'So what happens now? Are you going back to Africa?' Her question hovered in the air between them and for a long moment he didn't answer.

'Not Africa,' he said finally. 'I want very much

to be part of Kirsty's life, so Africa isn't an option, but as to what else…' He shrugged and the fact that he still made no reference to what they'd shared—*made no attempt to touch her*—hurt more than she could have imagined possible.

'You have to tell Logan.'

'Of course.' His voice was quiet. 'I was always going to tell Logan when the time was right. I'm going now. Are you coming?'

She shook her head. She needed space. She didn't know what she thought any more. 'You go.'

'I'll see you later.'

She turned to look at him. 'This is an island, Dr Walker. Of course you'll see me later.'

CHAPTER TEN

'CAN you imagine that? Being given the chance to patch up your relationship with your sister and then realising that you're too late. How awful. Fancy having to live with that. And fancy Catherine never even mentioning that she had a brother. It was obviously such a thorny subject.' Evanna carefully turned the chicken on the barbecue. 'Poor Ethan. No wonder he always seemed so tense, poor thing.'

'Poor thing?' Kyla stared at her friend. 'Aren't you at all angry? Don't you think he should have told us?'

'I think it's lovely that Kirsty has more family to love her. We don't all live life by the same rules, Kyla,' Evanna said mildly, reaching down and scooping Kirsty into her arms. 'We don't all behave according to one rule book. We're all different people, looking for different things. None of us is perfect.'

Kyla scowled at her. 'Stop being so reasonable. He took advantage of our hospitality.'

'Over the centuries Glenmore was often a place of sanctuary for strangers,' Evanna reminded her softly. 'We've always taken a pride in our hospitality.'

'But if we'd known who he was—'

'Then the welcome would have been warmer still,' Evanna said firmly, hitching Kirsty onto her hip and letting her play with a wooden spoon. 'I think it's very exciting for Kirsty to have someone in her life who knew her mother as a child.'

'I can assure you that the memories aren't good ones.'

Evanna seemed unconcerned. 'People are all a mixture of good and bad. Perfection would be pretty hard to live with.'

'Kirsty will get attached to him and then he'll leave,' Kyla predicted, and Evanna looked at her.

'And does that matter?'

No.

Yes.

She didn't *want* it to matter.

Oh, she was being so stupid. 'No, of course not. Well, yes, it's just that—I—'

'This isn't about Kirsty, it's about you. You're in love with him and you don't want him to leave. Have you told him?'

Kyla stared at her friend, wanting to deny it. But her mouth wouldn't form the necessary lie. 'Don't be ridiculous. This is a man who doesn't exactly communicate his feelings, remember?'

'That's him. But you *do* communicate yours, usually pretty loudly…' Evanna gave a grin '…so you should be telling him, just so that there is no doubt.'

Kyla raised an eyebrow. 'The way you're telling my brother that you're in love with him?'

Evanna blushed gently. 'That's different.

Logan doesn't notice me and he certainly doesn't love me. Me telling him my feelings would just embarrass both of us. But Ethan definitely has powerful feelings for you. I suspect he loves you, too, but you might need to nudge him into telling you. I'm willing to bet that he has no idea how you feel about him. At the moment all he sees is your anger.'

Kyla thought about the frantic sex they'd shared in the ruins of the castle. It had been primitive, desperate and… 'If he'd loved me, wouldn't he have trusted me enough to tell me the truth?'

Evanna removed the chicken from the barbecue and put it on the plate. 'This is a man who isn't used to sharing and trusting so, no, probably not.'

'So perhaps he's wrong for me.'

Evanna smiled and handed her a plate. 'Perhaps. But isn't it worth finding out?'

'He isn't like us.'

'And isn't that a good thing? The planet would

certainly be boring if we were all the same.'
Evanna poured dressing on the salad. 'Eat.
You're always cranky when you're hungry.
Logan will be home soon. He's up at the surgery
with Ethan.'

In the end, Kyla didn't wait for her brother to
return home. She felt restless and confused and
she needed to be by herself, so she drove back
to her cottage.

And then she sat for ten minutes in her
kitchen, looking out at the sea. And she still felt
restless and confused so she slipped her feet out
of her shoes and went for a walk on the beach.

It was only when she felt a hand on her
shoulder that she realised that Ethan was
standing behind her.

'I've come to apologise.' His voice was deep
and she turned, feeling her heart leap into her
throat at the sight of him. Would she ever be able
to look at him and not react like this?

'For what?'

'For making love to you before I told you
about Catherine. I certainly intended to tell you.
But this thing between us is strong—' He broke
off and she felt a twinge of disappointment.

He was talking about the sex, she reminded
herself. 'I'm sorry I shouted at you this morning
but I was angry with you.'

'I know. Justifiably so.' He didn't smile. 'And
now, Kyla? Are you still angry?'

'I'm not sure. I keep going over our conversations and wondering how many of them were
just about detective work for you.'

His hand dropped to his side. 'Is that what you
think? That my relationship with you was just
a means to finding out about Catherine?'

'You asked me about her in the pub that night.'
She shook her head in disbelief. 'She was your
sister and yet you were asking me about her and
I answered without knowing who you were or
why you were asking. And I can't help wondering if I said something that I shouldn't have said.'

'She was my stepsister and I wanted to find

out who she was,' he said quietly. 'I didn't know her. The woman I knew would never have settled in a place like this. The Catherine I knew was selfish and didn't think of anyone but herself. I wanted to hear you talk about her. And I wanted to hear you talk without knowing who I was because I didn't want my relationship with Catherine to influence your answer. I was trying to understand.'

'In that case, you should speak to Logan because obviously he knew her the best.'

'But different people see different things in a person.'

It was very much like something that Evanna would have said, and suddenly she wondered whether she'd been too hard on him. 'You want me to tell you more about Catherine?' She thought for a moment, trying to crystallise thoughts and images into something that would paint the picture he was looking for. 'She was— a bit wild, I suppose. She liked doing mad, crazy things. She flirted with every man she met. She was impossible to pin down and unreliable at social engagements. She wore pink shoes and high heels to the pub when it was pouring with rain and she never remembered to take a coat with her. But she was excited by life and enthusiastic about the island. She loved the beaches and Logan taught her to sail.'

'Was she pleased to be pregnant?'

'Oh, yes. She kept talking about family.' Kyla swallowed as she remembered. 'She kept saying that she was going to do it right this time, but when I asked her what she meant by that, she'd never tell me. I suppose I know now. Her death was a tragedy. It affected Logan very badly.'

'I can imagine.'

'She suddenly became ill but the weather on the island was so bad we couldn't transfer her for a few hours and the delay was critical. The hospital didn't think that the outcome would have been any different but Logan has always blamed himself.' She gave a sad smile. 'He hates obstetrics now and he always refuses to do home births.'

'You can hardly blame him for that.'

Kyla thought of her brother and her heart ached. 'I don't blame him for anything. But I know he blames himself. He carries it with him all the time.'

'Having seen your brother work, I know that he would have done everything that could have been done, and he did more for Catherine than anyone else had ever done for her in her life. I wish I could have known the Catherine that she became.' Ethan's voice was gruff with emotion. 'When I read that letter I felt a tremendous sense of loss. Not for what we had, but for what I sensed we could have had. Those early years were too traumatic for both of us and we were too young to be able to adapt. You describe a Catherine who was happy and yet I'd never known her that way. So I wanted to come and see for myself. I suppose although it was too late to change my relationship with her, it wasn't too late to alter the picture in my head. I wanted to change my memories. I wanted to understand her.'

'And have you done that?'

'I'm getting there.' He stared across the sea, his expression distant. 'I'm definitely getting there.'

'And you told Logan who you are?'

'Yes. He seemed pleased that Kirsty has more family.' Ethan's mouth flickered into a self-deprecating smile. 'Which just goes to show that they know me less well than you do. I'm not sure that I'm going to be the right sort of family for Kirsty.'

Kyla frowned. 'What do you mean, the right sort of family? Family is family. None of us is perfect but we all do the best we can and we're all there for each other.'

He turned to look at her. 'But that's the bit I'm not so good at, isn't it? Family, for me, has been no more than a word, but for you it's a way of life. Your family is reliable and sticks around no matter what. Your family shares. I'm no good at any of those things. I'm used to packing my bags and living where I want to live without thinking about another person's needs or happiness. I'm used to not needing anyone and to not being needed.'

Kyla looked at him, wondering what it must feel like to be so disconnected from the people around you. 'That sounds a lonely way to live your life, Dr Walker,' she whispered, and his eyes lingered on hers.

'It's the only way I know.'

'Feeling needed is good, and needing someone is good, too. For me, it's what life is all about.' She looked into his eyes and she willed him to kiss her the way he'd kissed her in the dawn light at the ruined castle. But he didn't move. He simply stood there, his eyes on her face, as if searching for something that he couldn't quite find.

And then he thrust his hands in his pockets and turned and headed across the beach and back to the cottage.

So this was how it felt, Kyla thought bleakly, blinking furiously to clear her vision. This was how it felt to be heartbroken.

Now she knew.

And the pain was worse than she could possibly have imagined.

'So that was it?' Evanna frowned at Kyla from across the best table in the café. It was right in the window and had a perfect view of the ferry and the quay. 'He didn't say anything about the two of you?'

'Nothing.' Kyla stabbed her triple chocolate ice cream with the tip of her spoon, wondering why she felt so totally flat and dejected. 'I really need to pull myself together. I'm being pathetic.'

'And what about you? Didn't you say anything to him?'

'What was I supposed to do? Beg?' Kyla frowned and lifted the spoon to her mouth, but the cold chocolate hit did nothing for her. 'I do have some pride, Evanna.'

'But he doesn't know how you feel.'

'I think it's his own feelings that are the problem,' Kyla said gloomily, putting the spoon down and staring out of the window as the ferry pulled away from the dock on the start of its crossing to the mainland. 'You said that the man had issues, and you're right. The man has issues.'

'And you're going to let that stop you?'

Kyla pushed the ice cream away from her. 'What do you suggest? That I hang a banner on the front of my cottage, declaring my intentions?'

Evanna grinned. 'In the old days you would have carved his name on your desk. 'K loves E. And Miss Carne would have put you in detention.'

'I feel as though I'm in permanent detention.'

Evanna reached across the table and squeezed her hand. 'It's not like you to give up. What's he going to do now, do you know? Is he leaving?'

'He hasn't said.' Kyla gave a humourless laugh. 'That would be giving something away, wouldn't it? And Ethan never gives anything away. I dare say the first I'll know of it is when Jim tells me he's driven that flash car of his onto the ferry.'

'You need to speak to him.'

'I have my pride.'

Evanna sighed. 'Pride isn't going to keep you warm on a cold winter's night, Kyla MacNeil. You need to think about that next time you're lying in the bed on your own, staring up at the ceiling. Now, eat your ice cream. If there's one thing a girl needs at a time like this, it's chocolate. Lots of it.'

Kyla was in clinic the next morning when Aisla came in.

'I came to thank you. If you hadn't thought that Fraser might be in the dungeon, goodness knows what might have happened.'

Kyla smiled. 'I'm just glad we found him and that everything was all right. Logan said that the CT scan was fine.'

'They think he has concussion. Apparently he might suffer from headaches for a bit and I need to keep an eye on him, but they don't think there's any serious injury. And Dr Walker looked at his wound this morning and seemed to think that it was healing nicely. I still can't believe he climbed down into that filthy, dark dungeon for my Fraser.'

'He's a brave man. A good doctor.'

Aisla sighed. 'He'll be a loss to the island.'

Kyla felt her mouth dry. 'A loss?'

'Well, he was only ever a locum, wasn't he? He was reminding me of that this morning when I was trying to persuade him to stay, but I don't understand it really. The man fits in here. I mean, why leave?'

'I expect he's leaving because we can't offer him what he needs.' On impulse Kyla stood up and walked towards the door. 'I'm glad Fraser is on the mend, Aisla. Call us any time if you're worried.'

She saw Aisla out and then walked into Ethan's room. 'What exactly is it that you need?'

He was seated at his desk and he looked up, his dark eyes guarded. 'What do you mean?'

'I don't understand what it is that you need.' Restless and boiling up with emotions that she couldn't control, Kyla paced the floor of his consulting room. 'I mean, it's all here if you look for it. You love to run and you won't find better anywhere. Or do you prefer fumes and tarmac to sea breezes and sand? You like to swim and we have a whole ocean waiting for you, or do you prefer chlorine and public pools?'

'Kyla—'

'Or is it the medicine?' she continued breathlessly, turning around and pacing back again. 'Because I can tell you now that you won't find greater variety anywhere. This island is like a small world. We have births and deaths and in between we have all the things that are part of life. And we handle most of it ourselves because we can't refer someone to the hospital every time things get slightly complicated. You'll get more hands-on experience here than you ever would in a London teaching hospital, and it's probably just as much of a challenge as Africa in its own way.'

He opened his mouth and she plunged on, afraid to let him speak in case he said something that she couldn't bear to hear.

'Or is it the people?' she said, finally standing still and daring to look at him. He was unnaturally still as he watched her, his eyes fixed on her face. 'It's true that everyone on this island is interested in everyone else, but that's because we're a community. We're not just a bunch of faceless individuals living isolated lives that never interconnect. We *care,* Ethan. We care in a way that you're never going to find in a city. We mind what happens to people. We care about each other and we care about you. I care about you. I love you, actually—' Suddenly awkward and embarrassed, she broke off, suddenly wishing she'd been born with some of his natural reticence because she knew that she'd given away far too much. She'd given away everything.

But then she decided that he'd probably guessed anyway, and remembered Evanna's words.

Pride isn't going to keep you warm on those long winter nights, Kyla.

He rose to his feet and walked round the desk

towards her, and she felt the steady, rhythmic bump of her heart against her chest.

'You love me?' His voice was deep and she felt herself backing away.

'Yes, but that doesn't have to be a problem. You can stay on the island and not have a relationship with me. We could—'

'Can we start from the beginning? What makes you think I'm leaving?'

'Something Aisla just said, about your post only ever being temporary. I know that this island is different to everything you're used to. I know that you're used to living your life very much on your own. You say it's the only way you know, but that doesn't mean you can't learn a different way if you want to. Catherine did it.'

'Kyla—'

'You *feel* it, I know you do. The magic of this place. I've seen your face when you run on the sand in the morning. I've seen the tension melt away from you when you breathe in the sea air. I *know* you love it here. And you care about the patients. You cared enough to dangle off the end of a rope to save a little boy from a dark dungeon.'

He brought his mouth down on hers and kissed her hard.

Her head spun, her knees sagged and she gave a little murmur of shock as his hands slid into her hair and he held her firmly, exploring her mouth with feverish intent.

When he finally lifted his head she blinked and tried to focus. 'That isn't fair. You shouldn't do that when I'm trying to concentrate. W-why did you do that?'

'I was showing you that I care about the inhabitants of the island.'

She swallowed hard, her hands still clutching the jacket of his suit for support. 'I'm just one inhabitant.'

'But the most important one,' he said softly, the hint of a smile touching his mouth as he studied her face. 'I had no idea that you loved me. That changes a lot of things.'

'You didn't know?' She felt her cheeks colour.

'You think I strip naked in the ruins of the castle for every man?'

'I certainly hope not.' He stroked his fingers through her hair. 'But I thought the fact that I kept a secret from you damaged what we had.'

'I was angry with you and hurt that you didn't trust me.'

He drew in a breath and his eyes narrowed questioningly. 'And now? How do you feel now?'

'Now I just feel miserable that you're leaving.'

He released her then and walked over to the window, staring out across the fields that stretched from Logan's house towards the sea. 'When I first arrived here, I wasn't even sure why I'd come. It was too late for Catherine and me, but I suppose a part of me wanted to identify the last few pieces of the puzzle. I wanted to understand what it was that had changed her and now I do, because it's changed me, too. This place restores your faith in humanity. This place doesn't allow selfishness because it's all about sharing. The island only works because people share.'

'I think that's what Catherine discovered. She said that she suddenly felt as though she belonged somewhere.'

'Yes.' He turned to look at her and her heart pounded.

'I thought you were going to walk away from me,' she whispered, trapped by the look in his eyes. 'I thought you were going to walk away from what we have.'

'Never.'

'But—'

He walked towards her and put a hand over her lips, humour dancing in his eyes. 'I think when we're married I'm going to have to gag you for part of the day or I'll never get a chance to speak and then you'll accuse me of being hopeless at communicating.'

Her heart almost stopped and she wanted to ask him to repeat what he'd just said, but his fingers were still covering her mouth so she was only able to make a 'mmm' sound.

His fingers brushed her lips. 'You're right that

I love Glenmore island. You're right that I love sea breezes and soft sand. You're right that I love to swim in the ocean, and it's certainly true that there's more than enough of a medical challenge here to keep me satisfied. And, of course, I love Kirsty and want to watch her grow up. But none of those are the reasons that I'll be staying here.' His gaze was gentle. 'I'll be staying here because of you. Because I love you, Kyla. I love everything about you. I love your warmth and generosity and the way you care for everyone. I love your slightly wicked streak and the way you love your family. And I want to be part of that family.'

He moved his hand from her mouth and looked at her expectantly, but now that he'd given her the opportunity to speak she discovered that the words were stuck behind the giant lump in her throat.

'Kyla?' His gentle prompt made her open her mouth and croak something incoherent.

'I didn't— You said…'

He lifted an eyebrow. 'I said?'

'A few sentences ago you mentioned…'

'I mentioned…?'

'Marriage.'

'Yes, I did.' He looked around his consulting room and rolled his eyes. 'I'm thirty-two years old and when I finally propose to a woman we're surrounded by medical equipment.'

'I don't care about the surroundings,' she murmured, hardly daring to believe what was happening. 'I haven't even noticed them.'

'Good. So is the answer yes?'

'You came here to find Kirsty—'

'I came here because I was drawn by the letter that Catherine wrote. Because I wanted to see this place.' His ran a finger over her cheek. 'But I'm staying because of you.'

'You're staying on the island?'

'It's going to be hard to be married to you if I don't,' he drawled softly, 'because it's obvious to everyone that this is the place you were meant to be. And, anyway, we have a responsibility to the community to have lots of sex.'

She gave a gasp of shock and glanced towards the door, but it remind firmly closed. 'Ethan!'

'Stop looking scandalised. You were the one who told me that the population has a duty to have plenty of sex and produce lots of children.'

She started to laugh. 'Yes, but—'

'If you're worried about the school closing, we'd better get cracking. If we start now we can have a child in every class right the way through primary school.'

'Ann Carne would have an asthma attack if they were all little versions of me.'

'But their daddy would be delighted. I can't think of anything better than living my life surrounded by ten little versions of you.' He bent his head and kissed her. 'I love you. And I'm looking forward to populating the island with you. Just say the word and we'll start straight away.'

'Ten? I don't think we'll be having ten.' She wrapped her arms round his neck, unable to control the happiness that bubbled up inside her.

'I can't believe you mean this. We're so different. You don't say much. Oh, Ethan!'

'I'll try and say more,' Ethan murmured against her lips with a smile in his eyes, 'providing you're silent for long enough for me to speak. Is it a deal?'

She loved the feel of his arms around her. 'Do you think you'll be able to stand living here, surrounded by islanders who want to know what you ate for breakfast and a big noisy family who frequently turn up to eat that breakfast with you?'

The smile in his eyes faded. 'The answer to your question is yes. But you haven't answered *my* question yet. Will you marry me?'

'Yes.' Her voice was soft as she reached up and kissed him. 'Of course.'

MEDICAL™

Large Print

Titles for the next three months...

December

SINGLE FATHER, WIFE NEEDED	Sarah Morgan
THE ITALIAN DOCTOR'S PERFECT FAMILY	Alison Roberts
A BABY OF THEIR OWN	Gill Sanderson
THE SURGEON AND THE SINGLE MUM	Lucy Clark
HIS VERY SPECIAL NURSE	Margaret McDonagh
THE SURGEON'S LONGED-FOR BRIDE	Emily Forbes

January

SINGLE DAD, OUTBACK WIFE	Amy Andrews
A WEDDING IN THE VILLAGE	Abigail Gordon
IN HIS ANGEL'S ARMS	Lynne Marshall
THE FRENCH DOCTOR'S MIDWIFE BRIDE	Fiona Lowe
A FATHER FOR HER SON	Rebecca Lang
THE SURGEON'S MARRIAGE PROPOSAL	Molly Evans

February

THE ITALIAN GP'S BRIDE	Kate Hardy
THE CONSULTANT'S ITALIAN KNIGHT	Maggie Kingsley
HER MAN OF HONOUR	Melanie Milburne
ONE SPECIAL NIGHT...	Margaret McDonagh
THE DOCTOR'S PREGNANCY SECRET	Leah Martyn
BRIDE FOR A SINGLE DAD	Laura Iding

™ MILLS & BOON®

Pure reading pleasure

1107 LP 1P Medical